Risky Business

By

J.T. Palace

ISBN- 978-1-7365854-2-9

Cover design by Meld Media.

http://www.meldmedia.net/

Edited and Formatted by Self-Publishing Services LLC.

https://www.selfpublishingservices.com/

Table of Contents

Dedication

I dedicate this book to my wife who stood by me, encouraged me, listened to me, and read my manuscript endless times, making corrections as necessary.

I also dedicate this book to my publisher, Self-Publishing Services, and my editor, Clare Wood, who persevered through the almost endless emailed questions, providing editing and guidance throughout the entire publishing process.

Preface

It was already dark when I drove up to the church on Eighth Street. I was about ten minutes early, so I decided to wait in my car and get the lay of the land. The area appeared deserted at first, but then a few pedestrians went in and out of the nearby restaurants and bars, and a few cars passed.

I mustered up my courage and stepped out of the car, heading directly to the front door of the old church. I opened the massive wooden door, entered the church, walked down the aisle, and sat down in one of the pews, about in the middle of the church.

After just a few minutes, a skinny man wearing a dark brown hooded jacket sat down next to me and handed me a folded piece of paper. I looked down at it and tried to read it, but it was quite dark and I could barely make out the words. All I could see were a few numbers and letters, as well as the words "Twenty Fourth Avenue main."

"This is all you will need," he said as I looked at the paper again.

I turned toward him and asked, "What does this mean?"

J.T. Palace

But he had disappeared.

The church was as silent and empty as it had been when I entered. I cautiously walked out, looking all around and behind me, and got in my car. I opened the small folded piece of paper again trying to figure out what it meant, and then I slowly drove home, not understanding what had just happened, let alone what was written on the paper.

How had I gotten into a situation like this? I knew running a business was difficult and unpredictable, but I always thought the hazards would be more along the lines of unreliable employees, a strong new competitor, managerial and financial headaches, and long hours.

But what was this all about now?

How did I even get involved?

Let me start at the beginning.

Chapter 1

The Real Stuff

As I stared across the large expanse of my desk at SMI, Inc. near the South Side of Chicago, I wondered why I had taken this new job when I already had a perfectly good job at the university. I enjoyed the work and my boss, and I was on campus all day, making it easier to attend my night classes for graduate school. Of course, this new job gave me an opportunity to move from the university/institutional world to the manufacturing world. Also, the pay was a little better, but, more importantly, it provided me with an opportunity for growth.

It was kind of funny how I had found this job. I was attending Latham Technological Institute in the Chicago area, working toward my second bachelor's degree in business, accounting, and finance, while attending another university working on my master's degree, all of which were classes at night. In my last year, I checked the job board at the university and found this one posted. As it turned out, the president of SMI was a graduate of Latham Tech and wanted his CFO to also be a graduate of Latham. Over time, I learned that business ethics was not one of his strong suits—but I digress.

I had called and set up an interview for the position. When I arrived, I found that this company was in a less than desirable area of the city. The Hells Angels motorcycle gang's headquarters was a few blocks away, a house of prostitution right next door, a steel "pickling" plant on the next block with all the associated toxic smells and pollution, and an abundance of boarded-up buildings all around. The dingy, one-story, red-brick building occupied the entire block, and a railroad track ran immediately behind it. It had electric steel overhead and walk-in doors, and I later learned that the only piece of glass in the entire building was on the copy machine.

I parked my car directly in front of the building, hoping it would still be there when I returned. After being buzzed through the electric walk-in door, I was led into a small office with cheap wood paneling and no windows. I was introduced to Chuck Fitz, a tall, thin man with serious breathing and wheezing issues, who told me he did not work for SMI, but for an affiliate. "Hi, I'm Jason Kirby here to discuss the open CFO position." "Good morning, I'm Chuck Fitz. I am very glad you could come in". At that point, after we discussed my background and resume, he explained exactly what the position entailed, the working hours, etc. Although I was apprehensive about the location, I felt it was a good opportunity. I would stay for a year or two and then move on. Little did I know that the year or two I had planned on would ultimately turn into over thirty-one years. But it didn't take me that long to learn what I had gotten myself into.

The office staff consisted of our secretary, Mage, who was a short, older woman with loose dentures and a gravelly voice. Mage thought she knew everything about everything, but in reality she didn't know very much. There was Rob, the inside and outside salesman, who was a tall, friendly, soft-spoken man with whom it was very easy to get along. He was a long time steel and automotive parts salesman who had no particular love for the family that ran the company (more about them later). There was Marty Gilbert, the plant manager, a tall young man who was Rob's nephew. Marty was diligent and hardworking, but he could not make a decision without taking an immense amount of time to contemplate every potential aspect of an issue, and that wasn't a good way to operate in the automotive industry, where things can change on a dime. Over time, I found out that he was also willing to do virtually anything to protect himself and his family and that he was out for only one person: himself. He had zero compassion for others, being a cut-and-dried kind of individual. He did well because he stayed focused on only one thing at a time, as long as that one thing fit his agenda of taking care of Marty.

J.T. Palace

George Roman Jr. was the president and was known as George Jr. or just Junior. His father, George Roman Sr., or simply Senior, was VP of sales and founder of the company, and his wife was the part-time bookkeeper. George Sr. had started a small company many years before, producing fabricated metal and welded parts for the automotive industry. That company had been sold to Gilbert Faustner, a local entrepreneur who had a number of steel warehouses in the Midwest and South and who had decided to vertically integrate several smaller automotive suppliers into his "empire" to provide additional customers for his steel warehouses and to give him an entry into automotive manufacturing. He had subsequently gotten into commercial and industrial real estate in the South and on the West Coast, often purchasing buildings on a whim, but he had retained SMI, although I was never entirely sure why.

Then there was Willy Roman, George Jr.'s younger brother. Willy was employed as the night foreman and had been married several times, having an abundance of girlfriends during and in between each marriage. He liked fast cars (including his Corvette), fast girls, and fast living. Much of Willy's time and money was spent on his Corvette, for which he ordered parts through the company, usually not paying the company back. It took me a while to learn that if he owed the company for some purchases that he did not pay for, I only had to go to Mrs. Roman, his mother, and she would give me a personal check to deposit into the company account.

Senior was an old "tool and die" guy in his mid-seventies, friendly and low-key. Junior was quite the opposite. He was short and stocky, very gruff, self-centered and arrogant, with a Napoleon complex. He strutted around barking out orders, drank heavily, and enjoyed being the "power figure." He had, for sales and entertainment purposes, a country club membership, a big cabin cruiser docked at a local country club, a luxury car leased for him by the company, and a virtually unlimited expense account for wining and dining customers. He was paid well and had all the benefits he could ask for. He was, however, greedy, and that ultimately led to his downfall.

Chapter 2

The Real, Real World

One day, I was reconciling some bills and saw an invoice for some special new tooling. I could not find a purchase order or receiving document to match.

"Ben, what is this twenty thousand dollar invoice for tooling all about?"

Ben Fanoto, the day plant foreman, only smiled back at me. I repeated my query.

"Ben, do you have a receiving document for this invoice?"

"No," said Ben as he smiled again.

I then went over to the maintenance supervisor, Fred McNamara.

"Fred, what is this twenty thousand dollar tooling invoice for?" Fred smiled and chuckled.

"Fred," I asked again, "can you show me where this tooling is located?" I showed him a copy of the invoice.

Again Fred smiled and spoke softly, "It's a new keel for George Jr.'s boat."

Twenty thousand dollars of company money was being used for a personal expense.

"Fred, do you know this company that it was purchased from, Nikko?"

Fred smiled again.

I walked away and put the appropriate notes on the invoice and prepared it for payment. As it turned out, Nikko and another vendor company, Mikko, were tooling companies only on paper, and both were owned by Frank Smyth, an old friend of George Jr.'s. The problem was that the $20,000 invoice represented a $5,000 boat keel, a $7,500 kickback to George Jr., and an additional $7,500 to Frank Smyth. In another instance, a $50,000 tooling invoice for a press die represented $10,000 of actual cost, and $20,000 of kickback money each to George Jr. and Frank Smyth.

In subsequent conversations over lunches, Rob, the salesman, confirmed these transactions. What complicated this issue was the fact that, at this point, Mr. Faustner, who owned one hundred percent of the company, was unaware of these kickback schemes, and they would ultimately lead to the ouster of the entire Roman family.

Ben, the plant foreman, was a short, friendly man who was diligent about his work and was concerned about the company's costs and operations.

Sometimes, however, he was not too rational about his attempts at saving money.

"Hi, Jason. I've got to tell you how I saved some money for the company."

"Really, Ben? Great! How did you do that?"

"Well, we needed some springs for the tool crib," he said, referring to an area in the plant used for storing tools and supplies. "They wanted an extra seven dollars and fifty two cents to ship it UPS. Instead, I figured I would save the seven dollars and fifty two cents, and so I sent Clarence, our driver, out with our truck to pick up the parts. I knew we didn't need them urgently, so I waited till he wasn't doing anything and then I sent him."

"Well, Ben, that is a great idea if we need parts urgently because UPS would take too long. However," I continued, "how far away is the store? About twenty miles? That's a forty-mile round trip. Our big truck gets about eight miles to the gallon, so that is about five gallons of gas, and at the current price of about three dollars a gallon, which works out to be about fifteen dollars. Now Clarence makes about seven-fifty an hour, and it took him about two hours to make the round trip, so that is another fifteen dollars. Forgetting wear and tear on the truck, Clarence's benefits and Social Security and other costs, the trip cost us about thirty dollars, which is substantially more than the seven dollars and fifty two cents UPS wanted to deliver the parts to us. Now, if this was an emergency, if a production line was down or something like that, then it would be a good idea for Clarence to pick up the parts or have the supplier deliver them. However, in this case, it's probably not such a money-saving idea. Does that make sense?"

"I guess so," said Ben. "I guess I never thought of it that way."

One day, Rob and I were talking about a few issues and he spoke about my predecessor, Rufus Connor, the prior CFO.

"He was a real slob," Rob said. "He had a beard that was always filled with particles of food from his last meal. He kept milk and yogurt in a file cabinet in his office, often for weeks, and then consumed the contents regardless of their condition, whether soured, stinking, or entirely spoiled. His entire car was filled with old newspapers and, unfortunately, he was not capable of producing financial statements on a timely basis, or at any time. He did nothing to enhance collections, improve efficiency, or reduce costs."

Rufus Connor had been let go some time prior to my arrival, and Chuck Fitz, CFO of an affiliated company, had handled the finances. Rufus had come along with the company when Mr. Faustner purchased it, and he had subsequently worked directly for Mr. Faustner, not for George Roman.

That was a serious sore point and had created considerable friction between Junior and Mr. Faustner, leaving Rufus in the middle, and Rufus was not capable of much more than filing papers.

The following summer, I took the first vacation I had taken in many years and went to a resort in Fort Lauderdale, Florida, for a week. A few days into my vacation, I received an SOS call from Junior.

"You have to come back immediately; the IRS was here and they said they need to do an audit and that we may owe hundreds of thousands of dollars in excise taxes."

I was already aware of the issue and it was not catastrophic. My predecessor had calculated these taxes incorrectly, tallying purchases instead of sales. I told Junior to relax, to call the IRS agent, and let them know that I would be back the following week to take care of everything. When I returned, I called the agent myself, explained the situation, and scheduled a time for him to visit. That visit turned out to be the beginning of a nine-month audit, but we were lucky for a number of reasons. First, the agent was a very nice, older gentleman who was planning to retire right after our audit. Next, he acknowledged we had no intent to defraud; but we had made an error in our calculations. Finally, he was willing to work with us, giving us credit for all the taxes we had already paid so that, in the end, the amount we owed was quite small.

That, however, did not prevent us from receiving a separate surprise visit from the IRS collections department, which was not such a pleasant experience.

One day, a large heavyset woman dressed in jeans and a dirty sweatshirt came in and said that we owed the IRS over $75,000 for past-due excise taxes, interest, and penalties.

"Do you know that the IRS audit is still going on and that no one has yet arrived at an amount due?" I asked her.

"I don't know nothing about that," she responded. "Just give me a check for seventy-five thousand dollars or I will shut you down."

I explained to her again that this was part of an ongoing audit, told her the name of the IRS agent with whom we were working, the name of his supervisor, the time frame we were dealing with, and so on, but she would not hear of it.

"I need a check now," she responded.

I was getting more furious by the minute. "Excuse me a minute. I will be right back," I told her.

I went to my office and called the audit supervisor, a Mr. Washington, and explained what was happening.

"That is the collections department, and we have nothing to do with them," he said.

"Don't you all work for the same agency?" I asked. "This woman is insisting I give her a check for seventy-five thousand dollars, and the audit has not even been completed. Please speak with her immediately," I concluded, calling her to my office and handing her the phone. After a few moments, she left without saying a word, but with an "if looks could kill" frown.

I got back on the phone with Mr. Washington.

"Do not send that woman back here again. I will not let her in the building and, in fact, I will report her for harassment!" I said.

He grudgingly agreed.

The audit was concluded after some nine months of review, back and forth on the amount due, and credits for amounts previously paid. We settled on a nominal amount.

That would not be my only confrontation with the IRS over the next thirty-one years!

Because the building in which we worked had no windows, when it was warm in the summer, we would open the large overhead doors to cool off the plant. A central air-conditioning system did a pretty good job of keeping the office area cool. One day, after Junior had returned from lunch, I noticed that the office area was getting colder and colder. I checked the thermostat and found that it had been set at fifty-five degrees!

When I went to speak to George about it, I discovered that he had been drinking pretty heavily at lunch, was "feeling no pain," and was very warm. His eyes were glazed over and he could barely mumble some words about it being very hot.

Later on, when it was time for me to go home, I found that George Jr.'s car had blocked mine in. At the time, a number of the managerial employees parked in the unused truck bays. He was asleep in his office, so I knew he was going to be no help. I spoke to Ben, the foreman, and he got a forklift, drove it over to George's car and lifted it out of the way, so that I could move mine. He gently put George's big car back in place, and George never knew what had happened.

As time went on, I discovered a number of questionable items, such as excessive unsubstantiated expense reimbursement requests, and internal costs that looked like (and were) part of the kickback scheme already mentioned, and I sent these with my regular weekly report to Mr. Faustner for his review, as he had previously requested. I was very uncomfortable about these discrepancies.

One day, Junior came into my office and asked me to become treasurer, with no associated increase in pay.

I told him, "no, thank you."

"Why don't you want to be treasurer?" he pressed.

"I really don't feel comfortable with the idea," I responded.

"You mean you don't want to get involved?" he asked.

"Yes, something like that," I answered.

The office atmosphere was getting progressively tenser; there were more discrepancies, questionable items, and transactions; and a number of other matters just "didn't smell right."

It turned out that I was correct in my assessment.

***

Not long after the request for me to become treasure, I received a call from Mr. Faustner. "We are serving George Roman and his family with court documents for a lawsuit for malfeasance and misfeasance, theft of company assets, and fraud today. I want you to have the building locks and alarm code changed, and to not let him or any of the Romans back into the office."

After I took care of his requests, I told Mr. Faustner that George Junior had a leased car that was in the company's name and for which we were paying.

"Can you get it back?" he asked.

"I will do the best I can," I answered. I hung up and called the leasing company and spoke with the person we always dealt with and explained the situation.

"Where is the car?" he asked.

"I really don't know. I can give you his home address and the country club address. That's about all I know," I told him.

"Where do you want the car delivered?"

I told him to have it brought to the office first and, after we inspected it, we would get it back to him to terminate the lease.

"How will you go about doing this?" I asked.

"Don't worry about that. You don't need to know," he said. "I will take care of it if you want me to. Shall I go ahead?"

"Yes, please take care of it," I responded.

Two days later, he called to tell me that the car would be at our office at two p.m. that day, and it was. I didn't know how he had gotten it back, and I did not care. I removed the overhead garage door opener and other items belonging to the company from the car and personally returned it to him, and he canceled the rest of the lease for us.

Chapter 3

Life Goes On

Now we were without a management team, and Mr. Faustner appointed Rob as general manager. Rob knew the products and customers for aftermarket sales very well, and he had a great rapport with customers, distributors, and suppliers across the country. He was, however, not an OEM (original equipment manufacturer)-type salesman. While he knew how to deal with the smaller, aftermarket customers, he just didn't have the "polish" to deal with the larger, more sophisticated OEMs. He had worked with Mr. Faustner for many years in several of his steel warehouses. Now, Mr. Faustner had brought him back in to run the company, knowing full well that he would ultimately need a good OEM person.

A year or two before, Mr. Faustner had worked with a sales representative who had gotten us a Global Motors contract. His name was Herb Henderson and he was an experienced automotive parts salesman. He had contacts throughout the auto industry. Mr. Faustner contacted Herb and persuaded him to become our general manager, and Rob was transferred back to one of the metal warehouse companies. Mr. Faustner told me how much to pay Herb monthly, but I was still to send copies of all sales reports, expense summaries, contracts, and other documents to Mr. Faustner on a weekly basis, which I did.

Herb had been in industrial engineering and, subsequently, an OEM sales representative for many years. I had many conversations with him about the company, including its direction and finances, as well as about the problems we were facing with regard to new business. I had also spoken with him on several occasions about the need for a larger facility in a safer location. Our current building near the South Side of Chicago was too small; it needed more parking, loading dock capabilities, warehouse space, and office space. Its location also made it difficult to attract good employees. Herb had spoken to the owner of the "hotel" (house of prostitution) next door, which a number of our production employees frequented after work, about the possibility of our purchasing the building and tearing it down for a larger parking lot, but they were not able to come to an agreement. Although the dilapidated building was worth only a few thousand dollars, the owner thought it was worth $500,000 for all the "business" income he derived from it. That immediately terminated the discussion, and we began looking for another location.

J.T. Palace

I found an old metal casting facility in a southwestern suburb of Chicago. It contained about 65,000 square feet—fifty percent larger than our current building. It was near major freeways, had plenty of parking, and included some thirty acres for future expansion. The facility was being shut down by its out-of-state parent company and its operations were being moved to Texas. The owners were eager to deal, and I was able to negotiate a purchase price of $450,000, which was less than the value of the land itself.

After we signed the offer, I asked Mr. Faustner what he intended to do with our current building. He asked me to sell it. I got an appraisal and Mr. Faustner gave me his sales price range, which was at the high end of the appraisal. He was intent on an all-cash deal, with no land contract. I contacted several commercial real estate agents, indicating I would not sign a long-term contract but would pay a 6 percent commission to whoever sold it for the amount we wanted. One agent agreed and ultimately found a buyer for $240,000, which was at the upper end of the range Mr. Faustner had given me. We closed the deal, received a check, and had ninety days to vacate the building.

After the deal was completed, Mr. Faustner complained, saying I should have gotten $300,000. I explained that I got the amount he wanted in a cash deal, not a land contract, and it was at the top end of the range he had requested. I also explained that we were currently paying $3,000 a month for a security guard to watch our parking lot, which amounted to $36,000 a year. The sooner we moved, the sooner we would save that $36,000 annually, and even more because we would not have that same expense at the new facility. In addition, I explained that we would be paying much lower property taxes at the new site. He then relaxed and acknowledged my position, and we subsequently completed both deals.

As moving day approached, we found we needed to accomplish a few very important things. First, we needed to "ready" the new building. That involved minor things like painting the office areas, and arranging for a new phone system and a new alarm system in the office area and the plant; and it included larger issues like ensuring the plant was heated. Because the facility had been a casting and forging operation, the former owners had depended on the heat from the forging furnaces for heat. Ours was a wheel production and fabrication facility that did not produce much internal heat, so we needed furnaces. We also needed to provide additional electrical capacity, improve the lighting, and upgrade the air-handling systems for the plant. Of course, we needed to find contractors to do all of this. We had to arrange for riggers (movers of heavy equipment) to come in, tear down, move, and set up all our heavy equipment. Most importantly, we had to build a "bank" of production parts, creating an additional supply so we would not fail to make shipments to our customers while we were moving. We could not afford to shut down production during our move. And all of this had to be done in ninety days.

To this day, the most amazing part of the move to me was the work done by the riggers. I found what might have appeared to be an expensive company, but they were the best in the Midwest. In reality, paying a little more for work that is done faster and with absolute precision is really a great savings. What I saw on moving day with my own eyes still seems unbelievable. The riggers came in, tore down the machines, loaded them on flatbed trucks, and moved them to our new facility, some twenty-five miles away, with incredible precision. It was a perfectly orchestrated operation. We were set up and running in twenty-four hours. In reality, we never skipped a beat. Of course, we had done all the electrical work, phone installation, HVAC, building alarm systems, painting, repairs, and such in advance, so we were ready to go the minute we moved in. Phones, in particular, were the lifeblood to our organization. Once all this was taken care of, it was time to make the new facility operational, and begin growing the company. It was no easy task, but we did what had to be done, and, in some cases, we did it at any cost.

Chapter 4

It Begins

Now our growth really began. Our employee numbers rose, and in some cases created quite a motley bunch. Our quality control manager was a fellow named Billy. Billy was from Smelly River, Kentucky. Billy was of average height and skinny, with half his teeth missing and a scruffy beard.

Billy had problems coming in to work on Monday mornings due to his weekend activities, which included many alcoholic meals.

At one point, as he prepared to get married for the fifth time, I asked him, "Billy, why are you getting married? Wasn't four times enough?"

"Well," Billy said, "I ain't got no money, I ain't got no car, I ain't got no house, so what do I got to lose?"

As strange as it sounded, he made sense in a very bizarre way. As time went on, we discovered Billy's strengths (of which there were few) along with his many weaknesses.

As business began to pick up and we found additional customers, we required additional production employees, additional equipment, and, most importantly, substantial financing. After we had moved into the new building, I established new relationships with bankers, insurers, attorneys, and more. I introduced myself to the manager of First National Bank, Chris Anderson, and discussed the company's banking needs, including checking, financing, and ultimately treasury services. He agreed to stop by in the next few days to continue our conversation and address our needs for these services. When Chris stopped by a few days later to continue our conversation, I explained that we needed additional equipment, a line of credit for additional inventory, working capital, and so on. He said he would get back to me in a week or two about the line of credit and promissory notes but that we could begin with a checking account.

A few days later, we received some bad news.

Global Motors Corporation, our largest customer, told us over the phone that they were seeing reduced demand and needed to cut back on their orders to us. Then we received formal documentation that Global Motors Corporation had suddenly lost 50 percent of its business as a result of intense foreign competition for certain products, and they simply did not need us to fulfill their prior requirements. Eventually, the slowdown spread, and soon we found ourselves reducing our headcount of production people, and cutting our orders to our suppliers. In what seemed like no time, we were down to just twenty people, from over one hundred working in the plant, trying to conserve cash and reducing unnecessary inventory.

We had to do this rapidly, so we would not be bleeding cash. Our bank would not want to provide financing to a company with such a substantial reduction in orders. Many of our costs were fixed, such as mortgage payments on the building, property taxes, and basic utilities. And all this was happening about the same time that Mr. Faustner was considering selling the company. The value of the company was reduced because it was thought no one would want to purchase a company that had no orders. Herb, however, knew that Global Motors would be looking for suppliers of over sixty new production parts in the near future. Because there was nothing in writing from Global at that point, we were all sworn to secrecy.

Herb got his wish: He was able to purchase the company from Mr. Faustner at a very attractive price, and promptly renamed it SMI Automotive. The acquisition involved some side purchases as well, in which we got accounts receivable and inventory in separate deals and were able to pay those off separately over time as they were used or collected. The deals certainly made it easier on our cash flow and made Mr. Faustner happy he was done with SMI.

I was not happy. Mr. Faustner had always been straightforward, fair, and honest with me. He did not like Marty, but he tolerated him because Herb liked him. Mr. Faustner was happy with Herb's abilities, but he did not care for him as a person or trust him, knowing full well his business ethics, having done business with him for a number of years before.

After the deal was closed, Mr. Faustner stopped by my office to fill me in on some details and to ask that I forward him all the appropriate documents related to the receivables and inventory payoffs on a monthly basis. I said I would certainly do so. I felt as if I had been sold down the river.

"Jason, you know I sold the company to Herb, right?"

Yes, I know," I answered. "What will happen to me and the rest of the office staff? You know that Marty is Herb's boy."

Mr. Faustner acknowledged he was aware of that, in some unrepeatable terminology.

"Jason, why don't you come out to Las Vegas with your family, stay at my hotel and spend a few days and relax? I'll give you a great room and we can talk."

I barely responded. My future was extremely uncertain in my mind. I told him I would let him know, he said goodbye, and walked out the door.

I did, in fact, decide to take Gilbert up on his offer. (We were now on first-name terms.) Several weeks later, my wife, my kids, and I flew to Las Vegas to meet with Gilbert. He owned one of the older, but still very nice, hotels on the Strip, and he provided us with a large, luxurious room.

Shortly after arriving, I arranged to meet him at poolside, and, for the first time, we had a relaxed, man-to-man talk. He thanked me very much for all of my work, my honesty, and the care I had taken in watching over his interests at SMI. He told me to contact him whenever I wanted and if I ever needed anything. I thanked him. That was the last time I ever saw him.

After a very difficult year or so at SMI, things began to pick up. Business was increasing, we had turned profitable, and we were expanding. Herb had named Marty as president, and me as chief financial officer and treasurer. Marty was responsible for the operation of the plant and the purchase of materials, and I was responsible for front-office operations, technology and office equipment, and outside administrative services, such as accounting, legal, insurance, and payroll. What did not change was the fact that Marty remained "Herb's boy" and was willing to do whatever it took to retain that position.

As if that wasn't enough, we began hiring. In the manufacturing area, we hired to meet production needs, adding a second shift and eventually a third. In the front office, we added a few people, but we preferred to rely on technology, so we computerized many of our functions, including billing, accounts payable and receivable, electronic data interchange with our larger customers, banking, and third-party technology for payroll, and benefits. Much of this was over the objections of our outside accounting firm, the principal of which felt we were usurping his powers. Along with this human and technological expansion came an eclectic group of individuals, some of whom tried to bring about the destruction of the company and others who, in their own way, added color and were concerned about the organization.

Shortly after Herb bought the company, he brought in members of his family and assigned them various functions. Not only were they not useful to the company, they were a serious detriment in a number of ways. Of his five adult children, his sons, Nate, Adam and Barry, were put in sales; and his daughters, Karen and Karla, in clerical and administrative functions.

Nate was the oldest and smartest of the bunch, but he had problems with alcohol, drugs, his temper, and female relationships. Adam was not very bright, and one of his greatest achievements was reading the phone book. Barry thought he was the world's greatest anything, and if you doubted that, you could just ask him. In fact, Barry would later almost destroy the company single-handedly. Karen was a pleasant, attractive woman who had spent way too much time in the sun and turned her skin into something very close to leather. Karla was serious and focused but not very friendly, and she acted like she knew how to do everything, whether she did or not. Neither was too enthused about working there and their work and attitude showed it.

After Barry had been at SMI as an aftermarket salesman for about two years, he was doing, we thought at the time, a decent job. But there were some issues with his methodology. One Tuesday afternoon, while I was working on a month-end report, my phone rang.

Herb said, "Jason, can you come into my office and bring your commission file with you?"

I grabbed the file I maintained that showed sales by customer and salesperson, as well as commissions payable and paid for the current year. When I walked into Herb's office, Barry was sitting there.

"Jason, can you review this year's sales and commissions for Barry?" Herb asked.

"Sure," I said, and I reviewed each of the invoices that pertained to Barry, including debits and credits. These were simply the sales made, the commissions due and paid to him, and any returns and charges back to his commissions.

Wait," Barry said. "What about the $10,000 invoice to Pennsylvania Truck? I deserved a commission for that. It is my account."

"You are correct, Barry, but they returned the entire shipment, so we had to issue them a credit and charge your corresponding commission amount."

"That's not fair," Barry insisted.

Herb explained that the action was completely legitimate because the company did not make a penny on the order, so neither should Barry.

Barry fumed but went on to the next invoice. "What about Miller Company? I sold them over fourteen thousand dollars' worth of material. Where is my commission for that one?" Barry questioned.

"Well, Barry," I explained, "you are right about the sale of fourteen thousand dollars on that invoice, but do you remember I told you at the time that I could not approve that sale since they had very poor credit and even worse references, but you went to Herb and had him approve the sale anyway? Well, they refused to pay even after several phone calls and letters, and I had to turn the account over to a collection agency and ultimately an attorney. So far it has cost us four thousand dollars in fees, and we have not seen even a dime of our money for our merchandise. It doesn't look like we will get any part of our merchandise back either, so you really don't deserve a commission on that sale. If, in fact, we recover some money, we can credit you for the difference above our costs, but that is about all," I said.

Before Herb could say anything, Barry got up and shouted, "I don't have to take this anymore," and stomped out of the office.

Herb looked at me but said nothing.

"Herb, do you agree with Barry?" I asked.

"Absolutely not, but we need to relax him," he said.

"I really don't know what else to do with him at this point, but you can take a crack at it if you want," I responded.

"Jason, I will see what I can do," he said. Herb had no clue as to what Barry would soon be planning for the company.

Just a few months later, after five p.m. one day, Amy, our senior secretary, came into my office with several sheets of handwritten notes from a yellow pad. Amy had worked at SMI for quite a while and was very knowledgeable about how the office ran. She was like a right hand to me as she knew where most things were, was very dedicated to her job and the company, and had no problem going above and beyond to get the job done.

"Jason, I just went to put some paperwork on Barry's desk and found this sticking out of the wastebasket. Please look this over right away," she said as she handed the notes to me.

I took a quick look and was astounded. Barry's handwritten notes explained his plan for taking over the company after he had arranged for it to be decimated. He planned to fire Herb, Amy, Marty, and me, and install himself as CEO. A competitor would take over all of our customers, and with Barry's help, run us out of business. Then they would take over completely. I told Amy to make a few sets of copies and leave them with me.

When Herb came in the next day, I went into his office and told him briefly about the notes and then asked Amy to come in to explain to him the circumstances of her discovery. We gave him a copy of the notes, and he slowly read them over. As the color drained from his face, he asked Amy to call Barry into the office.

She did and Herb said, "Barry, can you explain this to me?" as he handed Barry the papers.

After hesitating for a minute, Barry said, "Oh no, you don't understand; this has nothing to do with you or the company."

"Barry," I said, "this is in your handwriting and it's saying that you plan to take over the company and get rid of Herb, Amy, Marty, and me, and that you will be CEO. It is pretty straightforward."

"No, no, that's not what it means," Barry said, bumbling again and at a loss for words.

"Go pack up your office, get your stuff, and get out, Barry. You are done here," Herb said.

That timing gave Barry plenty of opportunity to pack up all his papers, files, and company documents before he left. Amy and I knew exactly what he was doing, but Herb could not bring himself to throw his son out immediately.

After that incident, Herb decided to expand our sales plans, and our sales force. His decision resulted in a series of errors, misjudgments, miscalculations, and what, in retrospect, were almost comedic decisions and events.

First on Herb's list was expansion from within. Adam was to visit a number of smaller after-market distributors in the Midwest, a trip that would take him on the road for one to two weeks through several neighboring states. We prepped Adam, providing him with lists of customers and their backgrounds, samples of products, and sales literature, and we made preliminary appointments for him. He got all his paperwork together and headed out. But first, he stopped at our company gas pump to fill up his car for the long road trip. Not paying too much attention to what he was doing, he filled the tank and drove away, neglecting to remove the hose from his car. As he drove away without looking back, gasoline from the now-ruptured hose sprayed in all directions, coating the parking lot and building. Our maintenance supervisor ran out, assessed the situation, and shut down power to the tank. He then shut down the valves so no more gasoline could spray out and ordered a new hose for the tank. Many of our employees had a nice show, but Adam was completely oblivious to the damage he had caused.

After his first stop, Adam called in to tell us, "This is not for me. I am not continuing on; I am coming back."

That was it. His big road trip was over, and he returned the next day. So much for a big sales thrust from within!

After that fiasco, Herb hired some outside salespeople. First, there was "Coach." Coach was an old friend of Herb's and a former hockey player for the Chicago Blackhawks who had long since retired. He had become an occasional sales representative for another company, depending on his name to get him into companies and sell products. That had not turned out too well for him, but Herb thought he would do a great job for us, with his well-known name getting him in to see potential buyers. After he was hired and given a "draw," an advance on his commission, it became apparent not many sales were occurring. He would come into the office every workday about ten a.m., have a cup of coffee, read the newspaper, speak to a few old friends or cronies on the phone, and leave before lunch, stopping to fill his car with gas from the company gas tank, and then be on his way. We kept him on the payroll for about a year but, after he achieved no new sales, Herb was finally convinced to let him go.

Next, we hired another salesperson full-time on salary. I had to take partial credit for this mistake, as Marty and I decided to hire him. Don Messer had worked for one of our major suppliers for a number of years, but his division was being disbanded, as was, ultimately, his job because our supplier was in serious financial trouble. Don had taken care of our account and was a good salesman. He knew us, we knew him, he knew our company, and we knew his, and he knew our needs in terms of products and was also very knowledgeable about the aftermarket automotive parts world. It appeared to be a match made in heaven.

It turned out to be a match made in hell. We did not know that his lunch usually consisted of eight to ten alcoholic drinks; that he had relationship issues that would spill into his work, including being married seven times and constantly having to take care of this ex-wife or that ex-wife; nor that he smoked enough to fill multiple ashtrays in a single day. When we finally got rid of him, we had to have the carpet and wallpaper specially cleaned to get rid of the impregnated cigarette smoke, despite installing an air cleaner in his office to contain the smoke.

Don had worked for Amalgamated Automotive, a major global conglomerate, in the motorized parts division as a sales manager. When we hired him, we explained his duties and what we expected of him. Everything was fine. But as time went on, it became obvious he was not bringing in a single dime's worth of new sales. He would, on occasion, come in with potential sales to some of his old customers at prices that were below our cost. Of course, we refused.

One day, he came into my office to complain about one of these potential sales. "When I was sales manager at Amalgamated Automotive, we did things differently," he said, rambling on about what a great job he had done.

I stopped him at that point, as this conversation had happened far too many times, and I said, "Don, because you did things this way, Amalgamated Automotive went under and so did your job. Yes, SMI is a lot smaller than Amalgamated Automotive, but we are still here and Amalgamated Automotive is not. This is the way it is going to be."

Don was not happy with my response to his temper tantrum, but I had had about enough of his boasting.

Don got along well with his customers, as well as with some of the women in our company. He frequently hit on some of them in his laid-back way of making conversation, showing how much he knew and telling stories about his many years in the business. He would start by simply standing around talking—a so-called water-cooler conversation—then with a quick lunch, and then whatever came after that on his and their personal time. This is most likely how he met his many ex-wives, but as they got to know his real personality, the relationships ended. As it became obvious that he was doing nothing to expand our sales or revenue, we had to let him go. He was costing us money—what with his salary and benefits, company car, and travel and entertainment expenses—and giving us zero return. It was time for us to move on and try to find a good salesman who would have the needs of the company in mind.

Risky Business

While all this was going on, I received a call from a man named Mohammed Al-Asmani. He said he was with Saudi Motors in Riyadh, and he wanted to come to our company to discuss a potential joint venture: manufacture of our products in Saudi Arabia and distribution of them in the Middle East. He was planning a trip for himself and his associate, Abdulla Qaatani, and he expected to be in the city in about three months. Would we be interested in meeting with them? I told him I would let him know in a few days.

Herb was open to the idea, and we determined some potential dates and discussed how he would like to see such a joint venture develop. In a few days, I contacted Mohammed and asked him to provide us with some potential dates for a meeting. He said he would get back to me shortly. I checked with our corporate attorneys, U.S. immigration, and others in preparation for what we might need or the approach we might want to take in setting up a joint venture with representatives from a foreign country. Once everything was arranged, we just needed to wait for our visitors.

It was not long before Mohammed and Abdulla arrived in the city, and the next morning, I picked them up at their hotel for our first meeting. Mohammed told me he had traveled with his wife, while Abdulla had left his wife at home. I offered to drop Mohammed's wife off at a local mall or store because she would be otherwise sitting in the hotel alone and she did not speak any English. He said she would be fine and that we could go ahead with our business.

On the way from the hotel to our office, we had some interesting discussions.

"Do you gentlemen have families back in Saudi Arabia?" I asked.

Abdulla responded that he did, a wife and three children. Mohammed also responded. "I have two wives and children with each one."

"How do you deal with that? Where do they live?" I asked.

"One wife lives upstairs and one lives downstairs," he responded.

I was shocked, but I continued. "How do you deal with all of that? Do they get along? What if you get tired of one of them? Can you divorce one or the other?"

"Of course. I just tell her to leave, and she leaves."

I was amazed, but I decided to end that course of conversation. For the rest of the drive, we spoke about our manufacturing capabilities, the parts we produced, what their needs were, and those types of things. We got to the office about ten, and I took them for a quick tour, introducing them to some of the office staff and Marty. We then went into the conference room to meet with Herb and our corporate attorney.

Herb made the opening remarks, explaining our company's background, current products, and manufacturing processes, as well as our quality control and the types of customers we had. Mohammed and Abdulla explained that they wanted to manufacture our products in Saudi Arabia, and with our assistance, set up a manufacturing facility there.

What was unclear was exactly what was in it for us. We pressed them on the subject, and they finally explained they would pay us for the equipment, setup time, and anything else involved. Basically, their plan was to pay us to set them up as our competition.

The project, as they envisioned it, did not seem too appealing from a business standpoint, as we were already selling our products in the Middle East through OEM and aftermarket distributors. This would be like shooting ourselves in the foot and being paid to do so.

They also told us we would need to send letters to the U.S. State Department and the government of Saudi Arabia acknowledging that we were sponsoring the project in a joint venture with them, even before we signed an agreement. With every additional sentence, this potential deal became less appealing.

We provided them with a tour of our plant, and I had one of our salespeople drive them back to their hotel. Herb, Marty, our attorney, and I were in consensus that we should not pursue this deal. That was the end, as far as we were concerned.

They continued to call and email, requesting that we send documents to the Saudi government indicating that we were involved in a joint venture with them. It became apparent that they only needed our name as a legal requirement in Saudi Arabia; they did not want us as a real partner.

One day, however, an offer presented itself that sounded worthwhile, though complicated. I received a call from our bank loan officer asking to meet with me. I agreed and set a meeting for the following day. Linda McQueen, our loan officer from First Ilinois Bank came in promptly at ten o'clock.

After exchanging a few niceties, she got down to business. "We have a company in our loan portfolio that has loans with us and is seriously underperforming. One of the loans was a line of credit, along with some promissory notes, and their payment history and financials had turned so bad, we terminated the loan, and they went elsewhere for a new line of credit to a lending institution that specializes in those types of high-risk loans. We still carry the two mortgage loans on our books and we really would like to get rid of them. At the same time, we think you can take over the company, make it work, and expand the operation. We would certainly appreciate it, and of course work with you on the financing. What do you think?" she asked.

I was a little surprised by the request and said that I would certainly be glad to look into it and review the company's financials, but I said that it would have to be worthwhile to us in terms of potential success, investment, and finances.

"Suffice to say we will be very generous in working with you so that we can both benefit. I will get the financials out to you right away and will be back to speak to you whenever you are ready," she concluded.

Linda had always been straightforward with me, and I knew I could trust her. I agreed to get back to her after reviewing all the information she would be sending me.

A few days later, I received her package with all the financials. The company was an automotive supplier and had done well until the owner decided to milk it and, as sales dropped, continued to take out more money for himself, to the point where it had become a less viable operation. Our review, however, showed that there were plenty of opportunities to cut costs, increase sales, and make the operation profitable over time. I discussed the information with Herb and Marty, and they agreed that we would make a decision after our outside CPA firm reviewed the company's financials and after we toured its facilities, which were about a forty-five-minute drive away. After that, we decided to go ahead, assuming we received favorable terms from the bank and Linda.

I called Linda in for another visit and explained that we needed assistance with the financing. She said she would provide us the same interest rate we had on our SMI loans, if SMI guaranteed the new loan and made payments of $10,000 a month. I countered that the prospective company, as it now stood, could not support those levels of payments. We would guarantee the loan for a short period, but we expected that it would be reviewed every six months and the guarantee would be removed within two years. We would also make the loan payments incremental, beginning with $4,000 a month for six months, then $6,000 a month for six months, and so on until we got to the $10,000 a month payments she sought.

She agreed, pending approval from her loan committee. She called a few days later, saying that it had been approved with our conditions and that she would be bringing out the documents. I told her that would be fine, but we still wanted to make a full site visit.

That was only the beginning.

The following week, Herb, Marty, our CPA, and I met Linda at the company for a walk-through. The current owner was not present, but still, we were astonished at what we found. The company had two buildings across the street from each other. They owned one building, which was being used as collateral for their loans, and leased the second. Each was about 200,000 square feet, with the first used for office and production and the second one used for production and warehousing. The owner had let maintenance slide, the production areas were dirty and in disarray, and the employees were doing the best they could in the current situation.

While some in our group saw all this as a negative, Herb and I saw it as an opportunity because most of the problems were fixable. The company also was paying $10,000 per month just to keep an outside line of credit available, in addition to principal and interest payments. I knew that just taking care of this one issue would be an easy fix to move the company toward profitability. This company was a diamond in the rough, and I knew we could polish it to its original luster with a little hard work. Herb wanted me to pay the loans off as soon as possible from SMI's cash flow, but after much discussion, finally agreed to keep this company completely separate from ours, letting it pay off its own loans and stand on its own feet. The deal was completed relatively quickly in accordance with our financial terms and conditions.

Then the real work began.

I made it a point to visit the new company, which we renamed SMI Manufacturing, twice a week for a few hours each time. What I found was hard to believe. They were doing computer runs to pay bills every single day. I changed that to once a week, and then to twice a month, freeing up the office staff's time, cutting back on overtime hours and costs, and substantially reducing paperwork. I also found that the healthcare offered to employees was minimal. The company was totally self-insured, meaning it processed and paid all medical costs on its own. With its older workforce, one heart attack could have brought down the whole company. This change also took incredible additional office clerical time to complete. To correct this problem, I had a health insurance company come onsite to sign up all of the employees. This took two full days, but when it was done, we had a fixed, manageable health care cost that greatly reduced exposure for our approximately 250 employees, and it came at a much lower cost. Following that, I had our quality control people come onsite and straighten out their system and put in tighter controls. I also had them install a new phone system that had broader capabilities and came at a substantially lower cost.

Then it was time for Herb to work on expanding sales. The company used a small, in-house staff and also an outside rep agency for sales. This was simply a third-party independent sales agency that handled sales for the company. The rep agency had been pretty much left to collect commissions on existing sales but wasn't doing much in the way of new sales. I arranged for the sales reps to come to SMI Manufacturing once a month to discuss the prior month's sales and their plans for the upcoming month. Just knowing they were being held accountable for what they were doing, or not doing, made a big difference in their attitudes and efforts to increase sales. In addition, I made it abundantly clear that they would only get additional commissions for new sales. That, along with Herb's push for more sales, increased revenue by 30 percent in the first year alone, and we had the company profitable within eighteen months. Then I pushed Linda to remove SMI Automotive from the loan guarantee. That was accomplished in less than two years, as she saw I had followed through on my commitment to pay the loan incrementally.

Chapter 5

Normal Problems

Over the course of a few months, we had received several letters from the Internal Revenue Service indicating that we had a balance due on our federal income taxes for prior years. I had forwarded these letters to our outside CPA firm for responses and did not think about them again. About nine thirty one morning, April, our receptionist and secretary, told me that a woman from the IRS was in the lobby waiting for me. April was a tall, middle-aged woman who had worked in transportation services in the past and had a very fixed, union mentality. She was extremely punctual, worked consistently, and was generally a dependable employee. At the same time, if lunch was from twelve to twelve forty-five, she began her lunch break at precisely twelve, not at one minute after twelve or one minute before. She never varied from her schedule under any circumstances.

I told her to send the visitor to my office. A few moments later, a small, slim woman about forty to forty-five years old came into my office. She was dressed in brown, a very conservative women's suit jacket and skirt, and white blouse.

Risky Business

"My name is Phillis McCarthy and I am with the Internal Revenue Service. I want it speak to you about your outstanding tax bill," she said.

Really?" I responded. "How much do you think we owe you?"

"The amount is right here on this sheet," she said, handing me some papers.

"Currently, it is nine hundred, ninety eight thousand, four hundred and sixty dollars, and ninety two cents."

"I do not believe we owe anything. What do you base your claim on?"

"Well, SMI Inc. owes that amount including penalties and interest due to a sales transaction."

"This is not SMI Inc. This is SMI Automotive Inc. What EID (employer identification number) are you looking for?" I asked.

"It's 38-8422753. See, it is right here on the letter."

"Well, as I indicated before, you have the wrong company name and wrong EID. Ours is 38-7536620."

"That can't be. It says right here that …"

I stopped her in midsentence and asked her to come outside with me. As we stepped out of the building, I looked up and pointed to the sign on the side of the building.

"What does that say?" I asked her.

"It says SMI Automotive Inc.," she answered.

"Now, what does your letter say?"

"It says SMI Inc.," she answered.

"So you see, you have the wrong company name, the wrong EID, and the wrong owner. In addition, when we purchased the company, we only purchased certain assets and liabilities of the former company, not the company itself. We do not owe a single penny to the IRS," I concluded.

"Well, I will have to take this back to our office to discuss. We believe you owe this money."

I repeated my point again, and she left.

This was the beginning of an eighteen-month exchange of letters between the IRS and me. At one point, I was sending packages of documents filled with yellow highlighted items to the IRS on a monthly basis to prove that they were wrong. Several months later, during all these letter exchanges, I received a call from an IRS agent in Washington, D.C., asking me who the owner of the company was. I explained who it was currently, and we again discussed the discrepancy in company names and federal EIDs.

"Well, where is Gilbert Faustner, the former owner?" the agent asked.

"I have no idea," I responded.

"Well, what is his phone number and address?" he continued.

"I don't know, and I don't care. I believe that is your responsibility to determine."

Several months later, we finally received a letter from the IRS showing that our balance due was zero.

Shortly thereafter, I was amazed to receive a letter from the state treasurer's office indicating they were going to do a sales tax audit and giving me the name and giving me the name of the of the state treasury agent who would contact me. On the appointed day, I received the call from Doris McGill saying that she planned on coming to our facility two weeks later at nine o'clock on a Monday morning to begin the audit. After a conversation with our outside CPA firm, I went about my regular daily business activities in anticipation of the treasury agent's visit. On the appointed day, McGill arrived.

She came into my office for a short briefing.

"I will need your current accounts receivable and accounts payable agings, and all outgoing invoices and payments and vendor billings for the past five years. Can one of your clerical people bring those documents to me?"

I took a deep breath and began. "First, I have an empty office prepared for you to work in. As far as the documents you are asking for, I want you to come with me for a moment."

I walked her to our records room and pointed to several standard four-drawer filing cabinets. "These filing cabinets contain the documents you are looking for. I cannot assign a clerical person to bring all of them to you. Check for whatever you want. If you need a few copies, we can make some for you, but not hundreds. Is there anything else you need or have questions about?"

After a moment of silence, she thanked me, and I walked her to the empty office that she would be working in. The audit went on for a few days, and at the end of the third day, she brought me a summary of her findings, page after page detailing what she believed we owed in sales taxes. The list was extensive, and the total sales taxes due were about $125,000, not including penalties and interest.

"Can you leave this with me? I will review it and return it to you tomorrow when you return."

"Ah … Of course. I will see you tomorrow." And she left.

I reviewed the multipage listing. When I was finished, I took a red pen and a ruler, and I put lines through over ninety-five percent of the listings. The next day I gave the listings back to her with my markings through them.

"What is all this? What are all these items with red lines through them?" she asked.

"Well, these are all covered by a part of the state tax code that deals with something called industrial processing, whereby a company purchases items that are used for the production process; these items are not to be taxed at the production level. Here, I have copied a portion of that part of the state tax code for you and will read part of it to you now:

"The State allows an exemption from sales and use tax for persons engaged in the manufacturing process. This industrial processing exemption is allowed for equipment, supplies and materials used or consumed in the activity of transforming, altering or modifying tangible personal property by changing the form, composition, quality or character of the property for ultimate sale at retail or sale to another industrial processor to be further processed for ultimate sale at retail. In simple terms, industrial processing begins with the first processing activity or machine and ends with the activity that produces the recognizable unit or product for retail sale or sale to another industrial processor to be further processed for ultimate sale at retail. The details of what constitutes the beginning and ending of the industrial processing exemption will be covered later. The theory behind the exemption is that if the end product is taxed, the components used or consumed in its production are not taxed so that the product is not subject to double taxation."

She sat dumbfounded, not knowing what to say.

"I will have to check with my office and get back to you."

"Certainly. You may have noticed that a few items do not have lines through them and those are the ones that apparently slipped by that we did not pay sales tax on and will be glad to do so," I said.

Later in the day, she told me that she had spoken to her supervisors, and they acknowledged my position. I would be getting a letter from the treasury department letting me know how much we owed. She briefly thanked me and left the building.

A few weeks later, I received a letter indicating that we owed $230.40 in sales tax, which we immediately paid. That was the end of our federal and state tax issues.

But it was not an end to our issues. There was, for example, Rachel.

We were growing and we were hiring. We were in need of production workers, forklift and truck drivers, maintenance/repair people, and many other kinds of employees. We always tried to hire from within when possible, offering employees an opportunity for a better job and higher pay, or we asked employees to recommend friends and relatives who would make good employees.

One such opportunity was for Rachel. She came in initially as a production employee, later applying for and getting a truck driver position, and later still, getting the opportunity to manage the tool crib. This was a secure area where we kept maintenance tools, supplies, nuts and bolts, and other such items that could be valued at a few cents each to several hundred dollars each.

Rachel was an attractive young woman, about thirty years old, short and sexy, with a personality that matched. Over time, Rachel was known to have slept with many of the male employees. This, of course, had nothing to do with her duties.

She did, however, get involved in some other issues. In addition to the items previously described, basic medical supplies, such as bandages, creams, and medical tapes were kept in the tool crib.

Eddie, the purchasing agent for the plant, had noticed that we were ordering an inordinate number of bandages and cotton swabs without a corresponding number of injuries. In just one month, we had "used" some twelve boxes of cotton swabs and twenty-two boxes of bandages. Our injuries were generally nominal, so something was wrong.

We had recently installed security cameras. They showed that on many occasions, Rachel had taken a large amount of cotton swabs and bandages and stuffed them in her purse. We confronted her, asking where the many hundreds of cotton swabs and boxes of bandages had gone.

She responded that she had no knowledge of any cotton swabs or bandages disappearing.

Then Marty asked her, "Rachel, can you show us what is in your purse right now?"

She reluctantly agreed, and emptied her purse in front of us. Out came hundreds of cotton swabs and bunches of bandages on Marty's desk.

"Rachel, what are you doing with all those cotton swabs and bandages?" Marty asked.

"I need them; they're mine," she answered.

"Why would you need hundreds of cotton swabs and bunches of bandages, and where did you get them?" Marty continued.

"I bought them at a store," she responded.

"Rachel, the tool crib is missing many hundreds of cotton swabs as well as bandages, and they are the same cotton swabs and bandages that you just emptied out of your purse," Marty continued.

"No, these are mine; I bought them a few days ago," she insisted.

"You know, we have a security tape showing you stealing these items several times. Do you want to see it?" Marty asked.

"No, but these are mine. I did not steal them," she insisted.

"Well, Rachel, you have two choices. I can either call the police and have you arrested, or you can return the cotton swabs and bandages to me, quit, and that will be the end of it. It is entirely up to you," Marty said.

Rachel took the rest of the cotton swabs and bandages out of her purse, pushed them across the desk to Marty, and walked out of the room, ending with, "I am out of here."

We never understood what she intended to do with the stolen cotton swabs and bandages, or why she would steal such incidental items, but the issue was closed and she was gone.

Risky Business

****

Amidst all the ongoing problems of running a business, particularly a growing manufacturing business, there are often things that add interest, intrigue, and humor. Sometimes these are small items, sometimes large incidents, and sometimes they have the potential to become large-scale disasters.

One day, a young man who was a production employee came to the front desk to fill out, sign, and turn in a new IRS Form W-4. This form allows an employee to tell the employer how many federal tax deductions are to be taken from his or her payroll check. It can be changed at just about any time by filling out another form.

April, our receptionist, called me and asked that I speak to the young man because he was making an unusual request. I told her to send him to my office. His name was Frank Evans.

When he walked in, I said, “Frank, what can I do for you?”

“Well, I want to fill out a new form so that I don’t have to pay any federal income tax.”

“Why do you feel you don’t have to pay any taxes?” I asked.

“I am a Native American and my friend told me I don’t have to pay any taxes,” he said.

“Well now, how are you a Native American?” I asked.

"My mother is one-eighth Native American," he said.

"Do you live on a reservation?" I asked.

"No, of course not," he said.

"Well, Frank, here is the deal. To not pay federal income tax, you have to be a Native American living on a reservation and listed as a tribal member on the roles of that tribe. You don't fall into that category, so you have two choices on this. You can fill out the form, put down as many deductions as you want, and I will turn it in to the IRS, and you can deal with them directly. Alternatively, you can leave your deductions as they are. Personally, I don't care which choice you make, but I can tell you that if you put down ten or more deductions, you will have to deal with the IRS and explain why you are taking ten or more deductions. It will most likely not be a very pleasant experience, particularly if they think you intend to defraud the Treasury Department on your taxes, but it is certainly up to you."

"Well, I'll take this home and go over it and bring it back tomorrow." He never came back.

****

We always had our December executive holiday party at one of the local country clubs that Herb belonged to, and we invited many of our better customers. This was a black-tie affair, with all the trimmings, including white-gloved waiters, a continuous flow of free alcoholic drinks, fancy food, a band, dancing, and on and on. After the first few years, I realized it would be much less expensive to buy a tuxedo rather than to rent one each year, so I did.

Inevitably, within a few hours of my wife and I arriving at the party, most people had imbibed enough to not know or care who had come, who was still there, and who had left. Herb always believed in doing things first-class, and these parties were no exception. It was just for our better customers, like Global Motors, and for employees of various government agencies. Although the party was relatively small, only eighty people or so, the bar and food bills were roughly the same, usually in the $15,000 range.

At one of these parties, I heard an interesting exchange between the parking valet and one of our guests, as my wife and I were waiting for the valet to bring around our car. It went something like this:

"Sir, what kind of car are you driving this evening?" the valet asked.

"I don't know. Hey, Helen, what kind of car did we bring tonight?" the drunken guest asked his companion, with a garbled voice. He was barely able to stand, and he was leaning on her.

"Honey, we drove the blue car this evening," she responded.

"We drove the blue car tonight," he advised the valet, who had obviously heard his companion's response. The valet brought their car, and they drove away.

I knew this verbal interchange would be repeated several times during the evening as many of the guests left. I knew what I needed to do. The following year, I arranged for two limousines to be available to drive people home. I made sure Herb announced to all present that if they felt even slightly intoxicated, to please have one of the limos take them home and come back to pick up their own car the next day. We didn't care how far away they lived; they would get a ride home at no charge. Although it was very expensive—about $1,200 for the two limos—it was a fraction of the cost of potential injuries and deaths, let alone potential lawsuits.

In fact, I can remember several occasions where one of us made sure people took the limos home regardless of their plans, just to be certain they got home safely and without incident. Herb and I were satisfied with this arrangement, and I slept a little better after this change was instituted.

The valet incident was by no means the only excitement. Picture yourself at a black-tie affair, with waiters in white gloves passing around trays of drinks in fluted crystal glasses, and a pre-dinner band playing soft music. Billy, our quality control manager, is talking to a few upper-level managers from one of our largest customers. He walks over to the bar and orders a beer. Normally at such an event, he would have had it poured into one of those beautiful crystal glasses. However, this former resident of Smelly River, Kentucky, chose to drink his beer from the can. Herb saw this and, as the color of his face slowly changed to a bright red, he quickly motioned to Marty to do something, Marty was busy trying to hide behind a table, having also noticed what Billy had done. Suffice it to say, Billy was not invited to any more of these annual parties.

Attending these parties was an experience in and of itself. Herb's kids, among others, would usually drink far too much, and they had a tendency to become overly friendly. Nate, for example, would speak to you in closer and closer proximity, until his face was just inches away from you.

Others would relax to the extent that they acted as if they were in their own homes or, more precisely, their bedrooms. One such guest was Bud Aarons, a former professional football player. Bud had been married three times, and it was often evident why. At one party, Bud had far too many drinks and let loose. The woman he had brought as his guest was of questionable background. She appeared to be what some might call a "working girl," or certainly a very close representation. As the band played, Bud hugged and squeezed his companion over her entire body. Some of us thought they were going to have sex right there on the dance floor.

The following day, I implored Herb not to invite Bud again. Because Bud was an old friend of Herb's, it was a difficult sell. But after he received a few phone calls from some other upset guests about this "performance," he finally agreed.

At yet another one of these parties, Adam's girlfriend, who happened to be very slim and tall, came in wearing what barely qualified as a dress. It covered only the briefest part of her body, so low-cut it barely covered her breasts and ending only slightly below her rear end. It appeared her dress was made out of a bathroom hand towel, and was about that size and type of material. Bud had brought his fourteen-year-old niece to the same party. Aside from the fact that this was an adult party, Bud had allowed his niece to come in a very low-cut dress, definitely not appropriate for a girl her age. Herb, his wife, and his sons and daughters all thought it was so cute. Most of the others attending did not. She, also, did not return.

Another regular event at SMI was the annual board of directors meeting and dinner. This generally took place in a private conference room at an upscale local restaurant and included Herbs family members and their spouses or companions, Marty and me and our wives, and our corporate attorney. In total, about fifteen to twenty people attended. Everyone would meet in one of the conference rooms, where Herb would provide a few introductory remarks, and I would provide a verbal summary of what had happened during the past year from a financial perspective and what we anticipated for the upcoming year. The briefing included a rundown of sales, profits or losses, balance sheet items, comparisons to prior years, anticipated capital expenditures, and any other major influences on the company's potential success. At the end of this discussion, Herb would hand out the bonus checks that I had prepared after Herb and I had discussed them. Of course, the family members were happy to get these nice bonuses regardless of what they had or had not done to earn them. Then their conversation would turn to high-level subjects, such as where they would be going to dinner the next week, what vacations they had taken, and so on. To a great extent, they all lived empty lives, with no substance at all.

At one meeting, the conversation changed. During this particular year, the company had done very well financially and the bonuses were particularly generous, in the thousands of dollars.

One of Herbs daughters stood up and said, “I think we should help all our production employees with some extra money this year to help them with their holiday bills, to purchase food for their families, and other things like that.”

I was shocked by her display of apparent benevolence and appreciative of her suggestion.

She continued, “I suggest we give each one an extra one hundred dollars.”

The shoe had been dropped. An extra one hundred dollars was going to help pay for food, bills, and gifts. On top of that, the money was not even coming directly from the family, or from their bonus checks, but rather was an additional gift from the company. Agreement was unanimous as they each clutched their substantial bonus checks and ate a sumptuous meal.

Had it not been so sad, it would have been funny. The display of “generosity” nauseated me.

Chapter 6

Stepping Knee-Deep Into it

One day, Herb came into my office and told me he had met someone who could get us a lot of money for the sale of the company. He was coming to see Herb that day, and Herb wanted me to meet him.

"Fine, just let me know when. I will be glad to do so," I responded. Shortly after lunch, Herb asked me to come in and to let Marty know to come as well. We went into Herb's office together, where we were introduced to Mack Davey, someone Herb had met during a card game at his country club. Mack was a heavyset man in his fifties, with a roundish face and red cheeks, and he had been a manufacturer's representative before forming his own "consulting" company. After exchanging pleasantries, Herb explained that Mack had met with some companies that had expressed an interest in purchasing a company such as ours. He said we could easily get somewhere in the $50 million range. This was far more that the value of the company, but I let him continue.

Mack said, "In addition, you would get the 50 million and actually get to keep the company and all of your jobs, and continue to control the company. Why don't we all meet for lunch in the next week or two and I can explain it all to you?" he asked.

Marty and I looked at each other, amazed by this ridiculous offer, but decided to wait for the lunch meeting to draw any definitive conclusions.

The lunch occurred a week and a half later at one of the country clubs to which Herb belonged. It was a smoke-and-mirrors spectacle. Present were Herb, his sons, Marty and me, our corporate attorney, and our corporate CPA. As lunch began, Mack explained how a company the type and size of ours was in demand by other manufacturing companies looking to expand their operations. Getting $50 million, keeping control of the company, and keeping our jobs was only the beginning. Shortly afterward, we would be able to sell stock in an initial public offering, or IPO, and secure at least an additional $100 million. I asked Mack to explain how all this would work, and he mumbled something about a public offering, spinning off the existing company, and creating additional companies and opportunities. He sounded like the proverbial snake oil salesman at a carnival, with lots of talk and no substance.

Herb ate it all up, hook, line, and sinker. Shortly after that lunch, Mack met several times with Herb in private. On those occasions, we always knew if there had been a major disagreement between Herb and Mack because Mack would come in with a box of doughnuts or a pie on the next visit to soothe the rift.

This game went on for several weeks until one day when Mack was there, Herb asked that I come into his office.

I complied and Herb said, "Jason, please prepare a $5,000 check for Mack as a goodwill gesture."

Herb knew how I felt about Mack and his proposal, and it must have shown on my face. "It's OK. Go ahead and prepare the check and I will sign it," Herb said.

I went back to my office and prepared a check to Mack Davey in the amount of $5,000. In the notation portion of the check, I added "ADVANCE ON COMMISSIONS."

This three-word notation would turn out to be a critical entry.

I returned to Herb's office and gave him the check, which he signed. I walked out of his office briefly to make a photocopy of it, and gave it back to him. He gave it to Mack Davey and Mack left. This same scenario happened several times, for a total of $25,000. Because I really did not trust Mack, I checked to see how and when the checks were deposited into his "corporate account." Each time he left our office with a check, however, he immediately went to the local branch of our bank and cashed the check. That told me he was a fraud and was living on our money.

In the interim, Mack told Herb about an Indian company that was looking to have a manufacturing company produce some product for them. Mack told

Herb the contract could easily be worth hundreds of millions of dollars. Herb apprised me of subsequent conversations with Mack regarding this opportunity, and I often voiced my opinion to Herb that this man was a fraud and a con man. I also told Herb what had happened to the checks that we gave Mack, and the results of some research I had done on him.

Herb dismissed my comments and disregarded my advice, and he continued to pursue this deal. It went as far as Mack telling Herb that the CEO of the potential customer company would be flying to the Chicago area, and he wanted to meet personally with Herb. This proposal was to be a separate one that Herb would do directly with Mack and, as such, Herb had advanced Mack over $1 million of borrowed (from the bank) money toward building a factory for this proposed production. Herb even went ahead and acquired a parcel of land.

As the day approached for Herb to meet the executives from the Indian company, Mack told him they would be bringing their private Boeing jet to the airport and parking it at Hangar 12. Mack even described the extravagant interior of the jet. At the appointed time, Herb drove out to the airport alone to meet with Mack and the executives from India. There was no private jet in Hangar 12, nor was anything else Mack had told Herb true. Herb even checked at various offices at the airport, and no one had heard anything about the plane, the company, the locations, or anything else Mack had told him. Subsequent checks found that the Indian company, the executives, and everything else was a total fabrication by Mack.

Herb was furious, and he told Mack to give all his money back immediately. Of course, Mack not only refused, he made up additional stories about other potential projects he was working on for Herb and the company. By now, Herb had caught on, and he threatened to personally arrange to enlarge Mack's rear orifice if he didn't get his money back immediately. Again, Mack refused, and Herb contacted our corporate attorneys to initiate a lawsuit in federal court.

I remembered that during one of our conversations with Mack, he had let it slip out that he maintained a home in Springdale, Illinois. I did some research and found the home owned by Mack. I verified the deed and ownership, and I had it appraised. It was worth $750,000. I contacted one of our attorneys and had a lien placed on the home and property. Next, I contacted our lead corporate attorney and told him to find the meanest, rottenest, dirtiest, slimiest attorney he could find to pursue this case. His response was, "I know just the guy." As time went on, we filed suit and did additional research that showed Mack had followed the same pattern with the owners of many other small businesses and their widows, whose husbands and families had built up successful small businesses. He was, in fact, a con man.

His unique twist was that he always settled any lawsuits just before he was to go to trial, so nothing appeared in any public record, and he never ended up in court. I explained all of this to Herb and told him we would get our money as the trial date came closer and after Mack found another "mark," or victim, to get the money to pay us off. I also showed our attorneys all the research I had done on Mack, including copies of the checks we had given him with my commission notation on the front. The attorneys said this notation would prove invaluable if the case got to court. After we filed our lawsuit, we received an invoice predated to a time before our lawsuit in the amount of $50,000 for consulting fees. Mack was trying to protect his position by calling his work consulting rather than finding projects, buyers, and so on, for which he would only receive a commission if he had been successful.

It was pretty amateurish, but it seemed to have worked in prior cons. We knew it would not work this time because I had kept the envelope with the postmarked date. Shortly before the trial date, our law firm received a letter from Mack offering to settle for about ninety five percent of what he owned Herb, and one hundred percent of what he owed the company, assuming we removed the lien on his home and property. After discussing his proposal, we decided that further legal fees would cost significantly more than pursuing the difference he owed Herb, and we accepted the terms and received checks for the amounts indicated in the agreement.

Herb never really apologized to me or even admitted that I was right about Mack Davey, but I was satisfied I had done the right thing and had ultimately saved Herb and the company a significant amount of money.

One would think that we were done with crooks and con men, but that would be an error. Not even six months later, Herb introduced me to Cal Donaven, who had been referred to Herb by Mack. I almost fell over, but Herb assured me Cal was OK and was going to make us all a lot of money.

I had no words and practically bit my lip off in amazement. Mack had put us through hell, and now Herb was turning to one of his recommendations. Cal had supposedly worked for several large corporations in sales, and then went out on his own, unsuccessfully. He appeared to be very knowledgeable with regard to import aftermarket automotive parts, but we were told little else about his background. Now we were hiring him to set up a separate, aftermarket import company. I knew this would be trouble, but Herb and Marty were both unconcerned, to the extent that I suspected under-the-table dealings but said nothing.

Afterward, Herb told me that Cal's salary would be an astounding $500,000 a year plus expenses because he would be traveling extensively in North America, South America, and overseas. I questioned him in private about this very large initial salary based on no track record whatsoever, as well as the large expense account, but he assured me it was well worth it, and that Cal was going to "make us all a lot of money." It was obvious Herb had been sold a bill of goods, and he probably would be paid off separately. I went ahead and set things up, and then I waited for the other shoe to drop. Not long afterward, Cal came in to tell Herb, Marty, and me about the terrific deal he had come upon. It seemed that Amalgamated Automotive was exiting another one of its businesses and was selling the inventory for "ten cents on the dollar." We had an opportunity to get these parts at that terrific price if we acted immediately.

"Fortunately, I have a friend inside of Amalgamated Automotive, and they can arrange for us to get this merchandise, so no one else would have this great opportunity," Cal told us.

I asked him how he knew the correct value of the material, and he told me that we would see the invoices and internal costs on the documentation when we paid. I also asked him how long it would take for us to sell this material to realize our ninety cents on the dollar markup and profit, and he assured me that within just a few months it would all be gone. Herb was elated, but I soon realized that ten cents was all the material was really worth, and Amalgamated Automotive and Cal knew that.

I had to set up an additional line of credit with our bank to pay the approximately $1.5 million for the material before we could begin accepting shipments. I gave all the paperwork to Cal and Marty to sign off on as each shipment came in before I would pay for any of it. New heavy-duty shelving had to be ordered, assembled, and installed to hold all of the incoming parts until they were sold. As the parts arrived, they were checked in and racked. As more shipments came in, the ten cents on the dollar became twenty cents on the dollar, and I continued to pay interest on the new line of credit until the material was sold. The "few months" soon became six months, and then a year, and the inventory of parts had barely been dented. No one wanted the material, as I had suspected, and that is why Amalgamated Automotive was so glad to sell it to us.

As time passed, I suggested that we lower the sales prices, even if it meant a lower profit, and we did. We sold a little more, but the bulk of it continued to sit on our shelves, and I continued to pay interest on the line.

That, however, was just the tip of the iceberg. I handled the accounting for our new import company, and I did not recognize the vast majority of the domestic vendors' names. That alone was not a big deal because there certainly were many such vendors I did not know. What did concern me was that I could not check on any of these vendors. They were not listed in the traditional financial resources, were not listed online, and did not offer references. Each time I questioned Cal about them, he told me that he had done business with them in the past and they were solid companies. I called some of them, checked with the local city clerk's offices, chambers of commerce, and state agencies that they would have had to register with and no information was available!

I knew something was wrong again, but Herb and Marty both were unconcerned. One company, for example, listed an address in Peoria, Illinois. As we were in Springdale, I took the day and drove over to the address listed on their paperwork as their office and shipping address. It was a vacant lot in Peoria. The following week, I did the same with another vendor whose address was listed in Bloomington, Indiana. When I arrived at the address shown on their paperwork, I found a drugstore. Adding to the mystery, I got an answering service every time I tried calling these vendors. The more I checked, the more dead ends I ran into.

But all this was only the beginning of my suspicions.

A short time later, I happened to be in the front lobby of our office when the mail person brought the mail. April, who would usually sort through it, date stamp it, and distribute it, had stepped away from her desk for a few minutes, so I accepted it and sorted it quickly to see if any checks or other important mail had come in. In the stack, I found a letter addressed to the National Bank of Cayman with Cal Donaven's name and our business address as the return address. The envelope had been returned due to insufficient postage. Because I knew Cal was overseas at the time, I took the letter into my office and gently opened it. I knew the old saying, desperate times require desperate measures. Inside was a personal check for $350,000 from Cal Donaven to be deposited in the National Bank of Cayman!

I knew now my suspicions were correct. I made photocopies of the check and envelope, returned the check to the envelope, and carefully resealed it. I took it out and put it back into the pile of incoming mail. Now I knew I had to work quickly. I left our office, contacted the FBI office in Chicago, and spoke to an agent, briefly detailing the events and my suspicions. Agent Robert Andersen, as he announced himself, asked if I could meet him between our office near Springdale and his Chicago office. I said I could, and we arranged to meet in a small restaurant in Urbana, Illinois, the following week.

Chapter 7

All the Dirt

I pulled up to the restaurant in Urbana the following Tuesday and walked in, recognizing Agent Andersen in the brown hat, suit, and striped tie he said he would be wearing. He introduced himself, as well as his associate, Agent Marilyn Parker. He reviewed what I had briefly told him on the phone and said he wanted to ask me a number of questions.

I told him, "Before we go forward, I need you to agree to something."

He nodded.

"I want to be kept abreast of your investigation, as I don't want to make any misstep. You need to agree to do so all along the way."

He nodded again, then said, "Tell me from the start why you originally had suspicions, what you have found to date, and where you suggest we go from here."

I detailed my first meeting with Cal, his referral by Mack Davey—at which time Andersen's eyebrows perked up and he cringed—the problems getting backgrounds on vendors Cal had found for us, the Cayman Islands check, and on and on.

Agent Andersen told me they had been following Davey and Donaven for quite some time, and they knew Cal had been involved in similar cons in the past, but they had never had enough evidence to arrest and prosecute him. This looked to them like the golden opportunity to do so.

I asked if he could find out how many deposits had been made into the Cayman Islands account and for what amounts, what deposits had been made in Cal's account and from where, and also if they could find out who the registered owners and agents of the various vendors were.

He assured me that they had access to resources that he could and would use, and promised to keep in touch, under the guise of an insurance agent named Roger Wilson.

I told him I would keep him up to date as well if any other developments occurred. I drove back to the office feeling that I was protecting the company but not sure who else at the company might be involved.

As time went on and their work continued, Andersen and Parker continued to keep me updated. They were able to access ownership records for the vendors and found, to no one's surprise, that Donaven and Davey were listed as agents in many of the state's records. This simply meant that they were listed as the principals of the organizations. Andersen and Parker were also able to trace $800,000 in checks that Donaven had deposited into the Cayman Islands bank account in the past several months. More importantly, they were able to track the sources of the parts that the vendors had been selling to us and found, by following the serial numbers, that they were stolen from large Tier 1 and Tier 2 automotive companies.

I was busy noting the overseas trips Cal was taking to visit our offshore import suppliers, and although I questioned Cal and Marty, I was never told who these suppliers were or exactly where they were located. I always received a vague response.

Cal hired an additional quality control person, who would stay overseas three weeks out of each month to make sure quality was consistent. The reality, as I was able to put it together from the bits and pieces I could find, was that this quality person was an old friend of Cal's who had a serious drinking problem that he called "not a big deal," and he really did not want to be home with his wife and children anyway.

As had become a pattern by now, each time I questioned Cal about his travels, I was stonewalled with useless answers. When I questioned Marty, he told me he did not know the suppliers' names. I asked Marty what we would do if Cal left our employ and we had to keep up the flow of parts.

Marty said he was not concerned and if it came to that, "Cal will provide us all the necessary information."

Not much later, Herb told me that he and our outside CPA firm were "very concerned about how I would be able to keep up with handling the accounting and finances for all our companies, and that it would be too much for me and too much pressure." As a result, the CPA would handle the accounting for the import company (the one Cal was running), and, I "would continue to handle all the rest."

This meant I had hit some raw nerves and was on the right track. I immediately contacted Agent Andersen and told him what had happened.

"We are definitely on the right track and are really irritating some people. Keep on doing what you are doing. We would normally pursue that avenue," he said, fully agreeing with me.

I asked him if he could possibly do some additional digging to see who else was involved. I wanted to know if Marty and/or Herb were getting checks under the table as well, from Cal or directly from the National Bank of Cayman. He said he planned to look into that as well.

I was pretty sure something like that was going on, based on their apparent lack of interest in the losses we experienced from the massive inventory purchase from Amalgamated Automotive, their apparent lack of knowledge about our domestic and overseas suppliers, and all the other little things that separately seemed insignificant but as a whole created what appeared to be a massive fraudulent scheme.

I soon got some answers to my questions. My concern about the continued viability of our companies was becoming more justified with each passing day. Losses mounted, we were burning through cash at a very high rate, and no one else seemed concerned.

Then came the important phone call. Agent Parker asked that I meet her and Agent Andersen outside the company. We again found a mutually agreeable location, this time in Decatur, Illinois, and we set the meeting for the following Thursday.

At the appointed time and place, I sat down at their table, we all ordered dinner, and Agent Andersen said, “Well, Jason, you were certainly right on this one. We were able to track large cash deposits into Marty’s and Herb’s local bank accounts, and corresponding withdrawals from Cal’s Cayman account. In addition, we found cash going into a bank account registered under the name of Mack Davey. We are at the point now that we will be putting all the evidence together and presenting it to a federal prosecuting attorney. I would expect we will know where we stand in the next thirty days.”

Hopefully, Davey and Donaven would be “out of business” in the not-too-distant future and would not be able to defraud anyone again. I would be walking a tightrope, watching everything that went on with Cal, Marty, and Herb, and at the same time not giving away my position or jeopardizing the investigation. It was nerve-racking, but I knew it would all be worth it when it was done.

J.T. Palace

I found it very difficult to go about my daily routine, interacting with Marty, Herb, and, on occasion, Cal, not knowing exactly what to say and what not to say, while trying not to accidentally leak what was going on with the investigation.

I knew the day of reckoning was coming, but I did not know to what extent, in what form, or exactly when. The latter was answered with a phone call a few weeks after my last meeting with Andersen and Parker. Agent Andersen called to ask when in the next few days Cal, Marty, and Herb would all be in at the same time. As best I could without letting anyone know why, I checked their schedules, and I provided that information to Agent Andersen.

He assured me it would be a clean and swift operation, and no one would know I was involved. On the appointed day, several agents from the FBI came into the office and asked to see Cal, Marty, and Herb, claiming they were with the Department of Homeland Security and were checking up on some employees. Cal came up and they all went into Marty's office. I could not hear what was going on, but I walked past the office several times as the agents showed their badges, spoke briefly to the three of them, handcuffed Cal, and walked out the door with him.

I found out later that they presented Marty and Herb with documents from the Treasury Department accusing them of federal income tax evasion because they failed to pay income tax on all the funds they had received from Cal; they were also accused of being accessories to fraud, theft, and money laundering. They were instructed to come to the FBI office on their own that afternoon to discuss the charges.

Herb immediately called our corporate attorney and CPA, and told them to drop everything and meet him at the FBI office. Then they all left.

I continued to act shocked, knowing full well that while Cal would be charged and most likely convicted, Marty and Herb would probably just have to pay the taxes due on the other income, along with penalties and interest. But I also suspected that Herb would arrange for the company to pay him and Marty an amount equivalent to what was owed, along with enough to cover the additional taxes that would be due as a result of the extra payment.

I also knew that, no matter what happened, it would be time for me to separate myself from the company, Marty, and Herb in the not too distant future. I felt leaving would be the best approach for me and for the company.

Now came some of the heavy lifting. Based on my current knowledge, my assumption was that Marty and Herb would be indicted and removed from the company—at least temporarily—so we had to first find an honest replacement for Donaven. I also searched for trustworthy CPA and law firms, ones that I could rely on and that I knew were not involved in anything that had transpired in the past. I did this without making the existing firms aware of the pending changes.

Marty and Herb were another major issue. Although they were principals and critical to the company's operation, they were ultimately proven to be accessories to Donaven's criminal acts, including fraud and tax evasion. As such, they would have to pay back all their illegal gains along with penalties and interest, and they were both put on an initial probation for five years pending formal sentencing. The federal judge assigned to the case, Jacquelyn Morris, also barred them from entering company premises, conducting any company business, or having contact with any company representatives other than for personal matters for a period of five years.

In addition, Nate and Adam were removed from the company. Barry—who had earlier been fired—was also barred, as were Herb's two daughters and his wife. That meant that by court order, I would be responsible for company operations while in contact with Herb and his family only by phone and mail. Judge Morris was very clear that we were to abide by these arrangements according to the letter of the law. Any variance would require her approval. While these were initial orders put in place by the judge, official sentencing would come much later.

I arranged for all the mail that Herb, Marty, and their families needed to be sent to them, as appropriate, by express mail once a week. In addition, I brought in some outside help to handle the day-to-day operations on an interim basis, as I knew I could not possibly do all this and my regular job duties alone.

I found a semi-retired CFO/director of purchasing who came highly recommended, and, after having him thoroughly checked out in terms of capability, honesty, and past ethical behavior, I hired him. Having done this, I became acting CEO.

Although I had thought I would be removing myself from the company very soon, at the urging of Judge Morris and our bank, I decided to stay on in an attempt to "right the ship" before it sank. I did not want the company to go under and all of our long-term, hard-working employees to lose their jobs.

After consulting with some highly knowledgeable and respected attorney friends, I suspended our existing law and CPA firms effective immediately. I found new firms relatively quickly from contacts I had outside of SMI, and they worked on extricating us from this mess and making sure the company continued to function. I brought both of the new firms up to date, and they both worked directly with the FBI and Treasury to seize the money Donaven had hidden in the National Bank of Cayman. Based on that situation alone, I was very satisfied with our new CPAs, Bill Peterson and Andrew Felps, as well as our new attorneys, Mitch Conner and Dave Jenson.

They were ultimately able to recover about $2.8 million of our money, which we used to pay some of the legal and accounting expenses related to the fiasco, to pay off the bank loans we had taken to set up and operate the import business, and to cover some of the costs associated with asset seizures. We did this along with the Treasury Department under RICO (Racketeer Influenced and Corrupt Organizations Act), which was made law in 1970. While the government received a good portion of this money, we were able to recover a sizable amount for the company as well.

****

While all of this was being put in place, the federal judge ordered that Marty, Herb, Nate, and Adam's salaries be cut by fifty percent effective immediately to ensure they didn't benefit from their illegal activities, and that any other payments to any family member for any reason be terminated immediately. This included any potential payments to Herb's two daughters, Karen and Karla, and his wife, Terese. I put that order in place and used the associated savings to help pay for the new legal and accounting representation and for the personnel I had hired to handle additional activities.

I guessed that I had five years to straighten out the damage that had been done, try to save the company, and get it growing again. I also had to manage operations on my own along with the new CFO, and I had to find other employment before Marty and Herb were allowed to return. If, however, I could not do much of this in twelve months or less, too much damage would have been done to our customer and vendor relationships to save the company. I, of course, worked closely with the new law firm and CPA, Internal Revenue Service, and Treasury Department as this was all coming together.

I was not sure to what extent any of our current customers or suppliers had been involved with these illegal activities, or to what extent our other companies had been impacted. I was depending on these new firms and the new CFO, George Montry, to help keep Marty and Herb out of any new activities.

I was expecting calls to start coming in from our export company customers and vendors. I had instructed the women who answered the phones to direct calls for Donaven, Marty, or Herb to my attention. I knew I would be able to get a sense of what had happened and who was involved by their questions and their tone.

Finally, the first of these calls came. "Hi, this is…" the caller said. "I did not get my check from Cal."

The FBI had recently installed a special switch on my phone that would allow me to record the conversation and also alert the FBI to listen in. I switched it on.

"Hi, I am Jason. I work very closely with Cal and have taken over his duties while he is traveling. I have worked with him for over a year now. Can you tell me exactly who you are and which check you are talking about?" I asked.

"I don't know who you are," the caller continued. "Can't you just look this up?"

"Normally I could, but our computer system is down now and we have IT people working on the problem as we speak. I will need to get all of your information and look things up manually in the interim, if you don't mind. If you could give me your name, address, phone number and email address, how much we owe you, and for what time period, once I can verify the information, I will try to get a check out to you within a week afterward," I said, making it all up as I went along.

"OK, my name is Harold Simms with Feneway Trucking, and Cal owes me five thousand dollars for the last shipment I made to him. It was the biggest shipment we made to him so far, worth about one hundred thousand dollars," Harold said.

"Please give me the shipment details, including the date you shipped it, what was in the shipment, and what the value of the shipment is, so I can look this all up and confirm it when our system is back up and running," I said.

I knew who he was because I remembered his name and his company name from one of the visits I had made to an empty lot. The money due was to pay for stolen merchandise that came in the original boxes with the name of the company they had been stolen from on them. Cal had the material taken out, repackaged in the import company's boxes, and shipped to a legitimate customer.

Mr. Simms provided me with the requested information, and I assured him I would call him back.

At this point, I checked the vendor in the computer system (which really was up and running), checked the location of the vendor to see whether it was a real location, and checked online for the vendor's background. Then I contacted the FBI to bring them up to date.

This was the first of several such phone calls that I took over the following weeks, but they helped identify the associated players in Cal's fraudulent scheme.

Cleaning up Cal's mess brought additional complications. As we eliminated the illegal vendors, we also eliminated our sources of wholesale material at below-market costs, and we would now have to replace them with honest, reliable, but more expensive sources. That meant the cost of the material we sold would be based on actual manufacturers' costs.

Now I would have to determine if these new, legitimate costs would leave us room for any profit, and, if not, how much I could increase prices without losing customers.

"George, can you come into my office? We need to discuss some items that need to be addressed right away," I said on the phone. George was a tall, slender man who had retired from his duties as CFO and purchasing manager with a medium-size automotive supplier. He was a very quiet man and with an introverted personality, but was very good at what he did.

When George came into my office, I began, "George, I have certainly kept you up to date on the situation with our customers and vendors. We need to find legitimate new vendors for our import company, probably some from overseas initially, that are already producing these products or that have the capability to do so, and establish relationships with them so that we can begin purchasing product and getting it into our pipeline. In addition, we need to negotiate new contracts with them at reasonable pricing, so that we can sell to our existing and future customers and still make a profit. Obviously, we were selling illegal product at stolen property prices with very large profits. Those enormous margins are a thing of the past now for us, but we still have to sell at a profit and retain our existing customers as well as develop new customers. Do you agree?"

"Of course. How do you want to begin?" he asked.

"I think we need to do a few things. First, I need you to find and hire a good, honest salesperson to maintain our relationships with our existing customers and to establish a new customer base as soon as possible. Next, I need you to find these new suppliers I spoke of and make those trips overseas to establish relationships with them, and get them to produce the product we need, if they are not doing so already, at the quality and price level that we need. I think I will go along with you on the first few trips to add legitimacy to the visits and to follow up on what was going on with Cal's suppliers there. I also want to take the new salesperson along so that he or she will have some background knowledge going forward on what we are doing and how we are doing it. Does this make sense?" I asked.

"Sounds like a plan to me. I will get started right away," he said.

"OK, find the new salesperson and start finding potential suppliers and planning the visits immediately. Time is of the essence, as they say. Keep me abreast of what you are doing. Thanks," I finished.

I then contacted the FBI and explained our plan and let them know I wanted some agents to meet us on our trip to follow up on the new potential suppliers to make sure they would be legitimate and also possibly follow the trail to Cal's old associates. I spoke with Andersen and Parker, and they told me they would take care of everything.

Not long after, we were all on a plane heading to our first stop, India.

Chapter 8

Following Up

We landed first in New Delhi. Neither George, Katherine (Katey) Sommers, our new head of sales, nor I had ever been to India, so the FBI agents helped get us through immigration and customs with the least amount of difficulty. They knew where to go and where not to go.

Katey, who had a lot of experience working with Indian and Chinese companies in the U.S., spoke the Indian and Chinese languages, and was familiar with many of their local customs. She was a tall, attractive, slender woman of about thirty-five to forty years old, with long red hair. She dressed in a businesslike fashion and had a friendly, outgoing personality, but she kept everything on a professional level. She was highly educated, pleasant, and I felt, just what the company needed now.

After the long flight, we went directly to our hotel, checked in, and went right to our rooms. As it was almost evening there, I immediately went to sleep, planning to meet everyone in the lobby restaurant for breakfast and visit the first potential supplier afterward. Katey had scheduled visits for us over the next few days with potential suppliers and one or two possibly fraudulent suppliers; the FBI agents would be along with us for those.

Then it would be off to mainland China, Taiwan, and Thailand. We had already set an internal company goal of three to four new qualified parts suppliers.

The first visit with one of the old suppliers was an eye-opener.

As we stepped into Punjabi Manufacturing and introduced ourselves to the receptionist, we were escorted into a small conference room. The FBI agents were presented as our purchasing consultants. Mr. Punjabi soon appeared, along with two assistants—tall, heavyset Indian men with ruddy complexions who stood with their arms folded across their chests for the entire meeting. It was a little unsettling, but, of course, the two agents were with us and that helped.

Mr. Punjabi bowed and introduced himself. I explained that we were looking for some additional suppliers and also wanted to visit our existing suppliers, so that as we grew and needed additional capacity, we would be comfortable that supplies would be available. He said he was very happy to speak with us and explained his past relationship with Donaven.

"I knew Mr. Donaven for many years from his work at previous companies. He was always very generous with his payments to us for our work."

"In what way?" I asked.

"You are aware of our agreement?" he asked.

"To some extent, but since Mr. Donaven left, I am not sure exactly how he paid you and based on what calculation. Can you explain it to me so, if we continue to use you as a supplier, I will know how to do so?" I continued.

"Certainly, we would obtain the merchandise from various sources, repackage it, and forward it on to your location to Mr. Donaven's attention. After he was paid by his customer, he would pay us from 10 to 20 percent of the merchandise value by check via express mail. The percentage varied, depending on the product, the urgency of the request and a few other factors. This worked very well for several years," Punjabi explained.

"Thank you. That is very helpful. Could you possibly make me copies of your and his documents, so that I can duplicate this process in the future for you? Unfortunately, after Mr. Donaven left, our computer system went down, and we are still trying to get it operating again properly. In the meantime, your copies would be very helpful for us to continue," I explained.

"Of course," he said as he made a quick phone call to an assistant. Our request was fulfilled in just a few minutes. The documents showed exactly how Donaven operated.

"Do you do manufacturing here at this location?" I asked.

"No, we just temporarily warehouse the products before shipping to our customers," he responded.

"So how exactly do you acquire these products? From other warehouses, manufacturers, or distributors?" I continued.

"Well, you have to understand how things work here in the manufacturing world. It is very common to receive an order—we call them requests—for certain merchandise, and it is up to us and our representatives to acquire this merchandise in various ways. Sometimes it is right from the manufacturers, sometimes from warehouses. These are not exactly what you in America call arm's-length transactions. We make an offer to our representatives, and they acquire the goods however they see fit."

We were certainly getting an understanding of how he and his company did business. The FBI agents asked a few additional questions, and we thanked him and left. The two large assistants escorted us to the door and outside to our vehicles. Their eyes remained on us the entire time, even as we drove away.

Our next visit went in a similar fashion to the one at Punjabi Manufacturing, with a similar description of their arrangement with Donaven and of how they acquired merchandise. At that point, because it was so late, we decided it would be best to return to our hotel and reschedule our third and last meeting in India to early the next morning. Afterward, we would take a one-hour flight to Kanpur instead of making the five-hour drive.

While this would be more costly than our original plans, we agreed that there were two compelling reasons for the change. First, word might be getting around with Donaven's suppliers that we were asking probing questions that might be exposing their illegal operations, leading these companies to take actions that could impact our safety. Second, time was of the essence in finding reliable and ethical suppliers to fill the void in our pipeline.

After we made the third visit, we could continue on from Kanpur directly to China. We all drove back to the hotel, feeling much more knowledgeable about Donaven's schemes, his low-cost suppliers that directly or indirectly stole merchandise based on the orders he placed, and his payment plans. It was much more obvious to us now that Marty and Herb were, if nothing else, complicit in these arrangements, knowing full well that the prices they paid for these products were well below market value, even without full disclosure from Donaven.

Donaven would simply pay the low prices he negotiated for the stolen material, siphon off a substantial percentage to himself—having the bulk of these "earnings" sent directly to his account in the Cayman Islands—and pay a small percentage directly to Marty and Herb to keep them content and quiet.

Back at the hotel, we met for dinner in the restaurant to discuss final arrangements for the next day, agreeing to meet in the lobby with our luggage early the next morning for the ride to the airport. George said he and Katey would make all the arrangements to change the flights and the meeting time with the last Indian company.

Our flight to Kanpur was uneventful, and we went directly to Rajendra Fabricating, which was located in a heavy industrial zone in a nearby small town. This company was not one of Donaven's former suppliers, and, therefore, it looked more promising. While relatively small, it appeared to be actually manufacturing, judging from the trucks loaded with raw materials, forklifts moving finished product onto the loading docks, and employee movements.

We walked to the building from the parking lot, stepped into the small lobby, and introduced ourselves. Our meeting was scheduled with Prema Chanda, CEO of the company. We were ushered into a nice, well-lit meeting room, with a long table and comfortable chairs overlooking the manufacturing area, which we could observe through a large glass window with open curtains, and we were provided bottles of cold water and glasses.

Chanda entered, along with Raj Pandu, whom she introduced as her CFO. Chanda was a very slender woman with a dark complexion, about five and a half feet tall, and about forty-five years old. She was dressed in modest but fashionable Western clothes. Pandu was in his early thirties, again dressed in Western clothes, with a white shirt, nice dark suit, and attractive striped tie. Chanda held both hands out together and gave a slight bow in the traditional India greeting of Namaste (namas-TAY).

"Welcome to India, Kanpur, and Rajendra Fabricating," Chanda began.

"Mr. Montry has provided your specifications to me in advance, and we have taken the liberty of producing some prototypes on soft tooling, preparing quality and testing data, and also estimated pricing for you. Before we talk about these, would you all like to take a tour of our facility, and ask questions of our employees, and then we can come back in and discuss additional details?" she asked.

We all acknowledged that would be fine and we began our tour. While the plant was relatively small, looking to be about 40,000 to 50,000 square feet, it was laid out well, with areas for shipping and receiving, raw materials, production, quality testing, and even a red area for parts that had to be further inspected before being released, reworked, or scrapped. We spoke with a few employees, most of whom spoke English very well, asked some questions, and completed the tour with Chanda and Pandu providing additional comments and explanations. We returned to the meeting room and Chanda explained the parts specifications and quality testing data. At this point, we discussed potential pricing based on quantity, frequency, and timeline, shipping and customs arrangements, and other such items. This was the first honest, aboveboard conversation we had had since arriving in India. We provided estimated quantities for each part number and also discussed what quality standards we expected, including testing frequency and other such topics. Chanda and Pandu seemed very comfortable with our requirements, and their pricing looked reasonable. We indicated that Katey and George would be in contact after our return to the States to discuss schedules and purchase orders. Having spent several hours there, we headed right to the airport for our flight to our potential supplier in China.

That planned trip involved flights from Kanpur to New Delhi, then directly to Shanghai, later to Nanjing and Tianjin, and later yet, to Taipei, Taiwan. The flight, including a connection in New Delhi, was about nine hours, and we were all pretty tired. Upon landing, we went directly to our hotel, had a light meal, and went right to sleep. We had agreed to rest for a day in Shanghai to get our biological clocks in sync, and then begin our meetings the following day. Subsequently, we decided we would leave for Taipei after our meetings in China and then fly directly home to Illinois, having postponed our proposed Thailand visits. It would be an exhausting trip but a necessary one and, hopefully, one well worth it.

I had, however, had a continuous, uneasy feeling since our first meeting in India that we were being followed. I could never identify anyone, but I was constantly looking over my shoulder. I mentioned this to the two FBI agents and they called in additional resources to cover our backs, so to speak, for the duration of the journey. The FBI's move turned out to be appropriate because I was not too far off base.

When we left Kanpur, a man boarded our plane at the last minute. I thought nothing of it until he followed us onto our next plane to Shanghai. The same person was joined by a second man, and they both appeared in the lobby of our hotel in Shanghai shortly after our arrival. I notified the FBI agents, and they told me they were already on it, having made calls to bring in additional people and resources. We all went on with our business, but I stayed in contact with the agents.

The first day in Shanghai, over breakfast in one of the hotel restaurants, we discussed our strategy for our upcoming meetings in Shanghai and Taipei. I noticed the same men sitting a few tables away, always in dark hats, coats, and glasses. They constantly looked over at our table. One was very skinny, medium height, and dark-complected. The second was slightly taller and a little heavier. They had now been joined by a third, larger man, who was dressed the same way. We finished our breakfast and headed up to our rooms to prepare for the day, as well as for our meetings that had been scheduled for the next day or two before we went on to Taipei.

As I headed into the elevator, joined by the two FBI agents, I noticed out of the corner of my eye that the three men sitting at the nearby table stood and headed toward the elevator. I hit the button for our floor and waited impatiently as the elevator doors closed and the three men approached. The doors closed before they could reach the elevator. We got off at our floor and went toward our rooms. The two agents, George, and I planned to do a little sightseeing and discuss strategy the next day, while Katey reached out to some old contacts in the area to help find potential suppliers or customers, as well as sources of information. We all agreed to meet for dinner that evening, again at a restaurant near the hotel lobby, to discuss the next day's scheduled meetings and any information we might have garnered.

The sightseeing was pretty uneventful, except that we continued to be followed by the three men at various times. They never tried to approach us but were always in the background. We returned to the hotel that evening, went to our rooms to shower and change, and met for dinner at one of the hotel restaurants. At dinner, we discussed plans for our four meetings over the next two days. Two of the meetings were with what we believed were former Donaven accomplices, and two with potential new suppliers unrelated to the fraudulent operations. At least two and sometimes three of the men continued to follow us wherever we went, although from a distance.

I decided it was time to confront these people and find out exactly who they were and what they wanted. I made that decision after our second day of meetings, before we left for Taiwan. The meetings were uneventful, with two small companies hinting at kickbacks to Donaven and, for the first time, suggesting they'd had a few conversations with Marty, although somewhat indirect. The FBI was very interested in these conversations and pursued them to determine if there was additional wrongdoing that involved Marty and to what extent he was involved.

I was in periodic contact with my office, and I found that Lance Douglas, the old CPA, had been trying to contact me, ostensibly for his own needs. When I finally connected with him, he asked to be put back on our account. I made it quite clear to him that it would not be appropriate for him to represent the company under the circumstances and that my decision was final. He then asked questions, supposedly for the benefit of the company as an ongoing concern and to complete his financials for the balance of the year.

The conversation was something like…

"Jason, how are you? Are you in town?"

"No, I am out of town right now. What do you need, Lance?" I was firmly convinced that Lance was complicit in the fraudulent schemes but did not have specific proof yet.

"Well, I just wanted to know what you would be doing about the current year-end since you changed firms in the middle of the fiscal year."

"We will be using our new accounting firm, as I previously indicated to you," I responded.

"Well, that being the case, can you provide me with current revenue and expense numbers as well as balance sheet and cost information, so I can finish up the current quarter statements?" he asked.

"Lance, as I indicated earlier, I will have our new firms obtain all the information that we need from you to do succeeding quarters and future statements.

The rest, they will reconstruct from our in-house records. Just send everything you have over to Bill or Andrew at the new firm. I have already provided you with all the contact information that you need to do so," I answered.

"Well, when will Herb and Marty be getting their monthly payments?" he said.

"I have provided them each a schedule for their anticipated payments. I have to hang up now, Lance, as I have a meeting to attend. Just leave things for Bill and Andrew to handle. They will take care of everything. Thanks. And Lance, don't push your luck," I said one last time and hung up.

It was apparent he was digging, at the behest of Herb and Marty, as well as trying to save his account, but I certainly was not going to provide him, or them, with any more information than was necessary. I had instructed Bill and Andrew about this, and I took similar steps with our old law firm and communicated that to our new attorneys as well.

When we returned to the hotel, Agent Andersen told me he and Agent Parker would check with the front desk to find out if the people who appeared to have been following us were staying in the hotel and, if so, in which rooms. The FBI agents were quite persuasive and received the information they needed. Agent Andersen provided me with the room numbers. We said our goodnights and headed to our rooms to get a good night's rest.

I got on the elevator and pushed my floor number, but as the elevator began its ascent, I thought about the people who had been following us and, as I become more infuriated and concerned, I changed my mind and pushed the floor for the room number Agent Andersen had given me. I decided to knock on the door and confront these people, and I'd find out exactly who they were, what they wanted, and why they had been following us for so long. In hindsight, that was not such a good idea.

I got out at the fourth floor and walked to Room 427, took a deep breath, and knocked on the door a few times. Suddenly, the door opened and as I entered, I saw the three people. One was the large Asian man of about thirty years old who looked like a sumo wrestler, wearing just a shirt and pants, his arms folded in front of his massive chest as he stared directly at me. Near him was a small person, maybe five feet tall and very slight, standing in a ninja-type stance and wearing a skintight leather outfit from his neck to his feet and a hat on his head, looking slightly toward the floor. The third man's big hat hid his eyes and forehead, and he was wearing a dark suit and shirt.

Before I could say anything, the heavy man took a fighting stance, and at the same time, something made of metallic silver appeared in the hand of the third man. Suddenly I realized that he had a gun in his right hand, raised, and pointing in my direction.

"Wait a minute," I said. "I didn't come here for trouble; I just want to find out who you are and what you want. You have been following me and my associates for quite some time."

At that point, the small, skinny man took off his hat and looked up, revealing long, jet-black hair and female features. She was a small, attractive Asian woman about twenty-five to thirty years old with a tough scowl. I was astounded, but not as much as I was by my next revelation. The man with the gun looked up and took off his hat. I was shocked to see Nate, Herb's older son.

I had not seen that coming.

"What are you doing here?" I asked.

"Yes, we are following you. It is your fault that my dad is out of his company and that Adam and I have had our pay cut," he responded.

"Wait a minute, Nate. You obviously don't know or understand any of the facts, and you did not see the federal indictments against your dad, Marty, and Cal. The source of the problem is not me, but rather the fact that Cal Donaven was dealing in stolen goods, skimming millions of dollars from these transactions and from the company, and sending them to a bank in the Cayman Islands. He was paying Marty and your dad from these illegal gains. In fact, you are very lucky that you and your brother Adam are not in jail over this. My job now is not to destroy the company or your family, but rather to rebuild the company, make it viable going forward, so there will be something for all of you to come back to, if and when it comes to that. All this, of course, was ordered by the judge in charge of the case. Now, why don't you put down the gun, and tell your friends to relax," I said.

The "ninja" woman did not seem to want to relax and Nate still pointed the gun at me, but suddenly, the sumo wrestler guy put his hands down at his sides and relaxed. Then the ninja woman relaxed, and Nate put his gun on the floor, looking very scared.

I was shocked and very proud of myself because I thought I had talked them all out of whatever their evil intentions were until I heard a noise, looked over my shoulder for a second, and saw Andersen, Parker, and two other agents, along with three local policemen with their guns raised. They quickly handcuffed all three and took them out. I thanked Agent Andersen and suggested he have Nate extradited to the U.S. At the same time, Agent Andersen said they planned to have the other two heavily interrogated to find out how they fit into the puzzle.

"Whatever possessed you to do something as stupid and dangerous as going to their room?" Agent Andersen asked me.

"I don't know; I just was tired of seeing these people following us constantly. I knew they were all up to no good, but I just had to confront them and get some answers. Quite obviously, in retrospect, that was not one of my smartest moves," I responded.

"Let's all go up and get some rest," he said. I got to my room, lay down on the bed, and shook almost uncontrollably. It was as if I had gone into shock. The events of the past hour finally hit me, and I realized how differently things could have gone, with a very bad outcome. It took a long time for me to relax, and when I woke up, sun was pouring through the window. I looked at the clock and saw it was five thirty in the morning.

I was still in my clothes from the day before and lying on top of my bed. It took me a few minutes to realize where I was and what had transpired the night before. After I mentally stabilized and understood where I was, I got up, took a shower, and dressed for the new day. I was a little slower this day, still reeling from the events of the previous evening. I went down to the restaurant for breakfast, but I was early, so I ordered some juice and read the Asian-English edition of the *Wall Street Journal* while I waited.

About an hour later, members of the group slowly began arriving. When Andersen and Parker showed up, they told me they had some preliminary information about the people Nate was with. The large sumo wrestler-type guy was a hired thug. I got another big shock when they told me the small attractive Asian woman was, in fact, Donaven's girlfriend. She had put Nate up to the whole scheme and had hired the thug for backup. Agent Andersen said he expected much more information would be forthcoming about these two and their scheme as interrogations continued. I was more interested in finding out how deep this scheme went; how many other companies and individuals associated with Donaven, Herb, and Marty were involved; to what extent, and in how many different countries these automotive parts theft schemes were operating; and a long list of other questions. Agent Parker assured me they would pass along this information as soon as it became available to them.

I was particularly concerned about obtaining more facts because we continued visiting existing and potential suppliers who may have been involved in the entire conspiracy. In fact, it appeared that Donaven, his girlfriend, and who-knew-who-else would stop at nothing to continue this massive illegal, profitable, and fraudulent operation.

After breakfast, we began our meetings with suppliers. As we moved from one meeting to the next, from factories in the city to those in the little villages, it was more of the same. We found it was easy to determine which suppliers were legitimate and which were part of Donaven's theft rings. As in India, some companies lacked manufacturing capacity and raw materials, had warehouses full of unmarked or repackaged boxes of parts and very few active employees, asked strange questions and made comments hinting at payoffs and kickbacks and orders from Cal. At others, legitimate companies manufactured their products, had active quality control procedures in place, had raw material inventory on the shop floor, and gave other indicators of their legitimacy.

We spent three days in China in Shanghai, Nanjing, and Tianjin, and then prepared for our flight to Taipei, Taiwan, where we would stay for two days and then fly back home. The entire time I continued to look over my shoulder, wary of every person who was watching us or looking at us the wrong way, and always keeping in the back of my mind what had transpired with Nate and the other two in Shanghai. I did not know how many more might be involved with Cal, or who might be following us or planning something worse for us.

We landed in Taiwan and were greeted by several representatives from the Taiwan police as we disembarked. They escorted all of us into a small conference room at the airport.

One of the officers addressed us. "I am Chief Inspector Chien Lin of the Taiwan Police Department. Welcome to Taiwan. I apologize for this unusual welcome, but we felt it preferable to greet you as you disembarked for your own safety and assistance. We are aware of the purpose of your visit, and the difficulties you had in mainland China on your very recent visit. We would like to assist you with your business here and help avoid any of the complications or incidents you experienced a few days ago. Agents Andersen and Parker have already provided us with the list of your planned visits to the various potential suppliers, and we would like to accompany you on these visits, as well as to your hotel for your own protection. We also are trying to find and apprehend members of the large Asian theft ring you have apparently come in contact with and disrupted, and note that you have been quite successful in identifying some of these people already. Are there any questions?"

We indicated that we had none, and with that, the inspector said his department would assist us through customs and immigration control, and escort us to our hotel in unmarked vehicles.

"Inspector, I want to thank you very much for this assistance and want you to know we understand the importance of your mission and appreciate any assistance you can offer," I said. "At the same time, we want you to understand the primary purpose of our visit is to find local qualified and ethical suppliers for our company, and we do not want that purpose to be compromised in any way."

With that, we all left the conference room, retrieved our luggage, and traveled to our hotel. Our group checked in and met two hours later for dinner in the hotel restaurant. Katey and George had scheduled two days of meetings with potential suppliers, so we discussed what we knew about the companies in terms of strengths and weaknesses, their potential for manufacturing the products we needed, and any information we had regarding their assumed honesty. Our first meeting was scheduled for nine o'clock the next morning, so we adjourned to our rooms to prepare business strategy and get some rest so we could get an early start. We decided to meet in the lobby of the hotel at eight o'clock in the morning.

I asked Inspector Lin to dress himself and his associates in plainclothes when they accompanied us, and we would introduce them as members of our consulting staff from Taiwan, so as not to draw too much attention to them. He agreed and was happy to be involved in the visits.

The next morning, we all met in the lobby at eight o'clock sharp. The inspector and two of his staff were also present in plainclothes with plain, unmarked vehicles. We left for the day's visits, and the first company appeared to be viable in terms of manufacturing expertise, quality, and volume, but the second one was questionable. As had happened in India and China, we found no manufacturing capability at all, just a large warehouse with racked boxes and a small production line for printing and numbering them. When we asked representatives of the company about their manufacturing expertise, we were told that those functions took place at other locations. We obtained the addresses of those immediately. The two companies we visited the next day looked OK, although one did not have the capabilities we were looking for. We returned to the hotel in the afternoon of the second day, planned a debriefing meeting, and prepared to depart for the airport the next morning.

Inspector Lin indicated he would come an hour early to the hotel to give us the results of his investigation of the second company from our first day's visit, and to accompany us to the airport to help expedite our movement through the various inspections, so we could board our flight home easily. I thanked him, and, George, Katey, and I met in the hotel restaurant for dinner and discussion.

J.T. Palace

In the morning, we came down to breakfast before leaving, and Inspector Lin was waiting for us in the hotel restaurant.

As we sat down to eat, he began: "We investigated the company we met with on the first day that we were all concerned about. Several people from my staff went to the purported manufacturing sites they gave us, only to find either empty land or homes. In no case did we find any manufacturing facilities. In addition, we checked on the ownership of this company, and we found it is associated with known criminal elements. We will be pursuing this company and bringing them through our criminal justice system, investigating further for fraud and theft. We do appreciate your help in identifying this company and allowing us to accompany you on the visit. I hope you consider your time in Taiwan worthwhile and hope you will return and do business with companies in our country."

Before I had an opportunity to respond, FBI Agent Andersen said, "Thank you very much, Inspector Lin. Our local agents will be working with you on this investigation, and we certainly appreciate your assistance on this part of our trip."

I added, "We really appreciated your assistance from the time we landed through our intended departure, and we also appreciate your working with us with in regard to not identifying yourselves as police officers and for helping us expedite our movement in and out of Taiwan. I look forward to being in contact with you in the future, and I will certainly give every consideration to local companies becoming suppliers of SMI for our manufacturing needs."

We boarded the plane and took our seats. I contemplated the entirety of our trip and all that occurred, and thought about what awaited us upon our return, all while the plane taxied and took off. While I was still deep in my thoughts, the plane had leveled off at cruising speed for the long trip back to the U.S. George came up the aisle and sat next to me in an empty seat.

I was still deep in thought when George started talking. "Interesting trip, huh?"

I was a little startled until I realized where I was and who was speaking to me. "Well, George, I think we accomplished a great deal in a relatively short time, and we know better who and what we are dealing with. We also made some good contacts for potential suppliers, so I think it was quite successful, despite the little bumps in the road, so to speak. Now we really have our work cut out for us."

"What do you mean?" asked George.

"Well," I said, "we need to thoroughly clear the potential vendors that we liked to make sure they can provide us with the product we need, the quality and quantity we need, and a price we can make work for us. Then we will need to request production samples, and finally production runs, if everything looks good. More importantly, we need to figure out how to keep our existing customers with the higher prices we will likely need to charge them now that we will be purchasing legitimately manufactured instead of stolen merchandise. As soon we get back, I want to meet with you and Katey to set strategy and make short- and long-term plans. If you have any thoughts on this, I would certainly like to hear them, either now, or at our first meeting after we get back," I finished.

"Well, I do have a few thoughts, but I want to speak to Katey first. Do you mind if we discuss all this after we get back, after I have time to digest all that has happened and have a conversation with Katey about it?" George asked.

"That will be fine. Let's schedule a meeting for a day or so after we return, after we catch up with pressing business. Then we can discuss this and talk about our next moves and get started on our game plan. We will, however, need to move fast so that we don't lose our existing customer base, and, at the same time, position the company for growth and guarantee sufficient cash flow and financing. I will also need you to schedule meetings with our new law firm and CPA firm, as well as our bankers, to make sure they are up to date and know where we are with all of this, and what our intentions are. They will be helping us along the way and pointing out any potential hazards," I said.

"Sounds like a plan. I'll get started as soon as we return," said George as he returned to his seat.

I was almost immediately lost in thought again, and I did not realize I had fallen asleep for several hours until the flight attendant gently nudged me to see if I wanted breakfast. I agreed to the breakfast and a few minutes later, Agent Andersen came up to sit next to me.

I asked him what he anticipated our former colleagues might have in store for them.

"Well, I cannot give you an answer with any certainty," he said. "But based on my experience and knowledge of past history, I would guess that in the case of Herb and Marty, the best-case scenario would be taxes on any illegal earnings, that is, the money they made on the sales of the stolen merchandise, and heavy penalties and interest from the IRS as well. Worst-case scenario would be for both of them to face criminal action and possibly jail time. With Cal, I would seriously guess that he will be paying taxes on all his illegal earnings, penalties and interest to the IRS, as well as a very good likelihood that he will be facing time in jail. Obviously there is no certainty in what I am telling you, but that is my opinion."

"Thanks. That pretty much falls in line with my guess as well," I said. "After we land, I will be pretty busy at work, trying to get our new plans in place, use all the information we obtained from this trip, and engage in a series of meetings with my staff and outside third parties. I would, however, like you to continue to keep me up to date on what you find out relative to the companies and individuals involved in these stolen auto parts rings, and any other information you may obtain about other similar companies, so we do not run into this problem again with other potential vendors," I said.

"No problem. I would be glad to keep in touch. You and your colleagues have been extremely open and helpful in this investigation, and I and the bureau would be more than happy to assist," he said.

He went back to his seat, and I finished my breakfast and briefly fell asleep again, only to be awakened by the pilot announcing that we were beginning our final approach to the airport just outside of Chicago.

Chapter 9

Back to the Real World, the Real Work, and the Real Truth

It was a little cool but sunny when we landed, disembarked the airplane, and went down to retrieve our luggage. Then we drove back to Springdale, while Andersen and Parker drove to Chicago. I decided to go directly home to relax before the next day, when I would tackle the mass of problems and issues this trip had generated, as well as any new problems that had come up. The next morning came too soon, but I got into the office before seven a.m., conferred with Amy and April about any pressing problems, and then met with Billy to see if there were any urgent needs before I met with George and Katey.

Billy said one of our products had been rejected by our largest customer, Global Motors. He had not been able to determine the root cause, but Global Motors had put us on containment as of the day before. Containment is a costly and time-consuming process whereby we must send every single part we manufacture to a third-party vendor that our customer has chosen to inspect each and every part and return to us any and all defective parts for remediation or scrap. The cost to us is very high in terms of cost of the third-party inspection, delay in shipping parts to our customer, and impact on our name in our customer's eyes.

"Billy, briefly explain the problem to me as you see it," I said.

"Well, on Monday afternoon I got a call from my contact at Global Motors Plant Number 3 indicating that our wheels were not fitting their vehicles properly."

"Were all these parts from the same lot, from all of their shifts, or just some of them?" I asked.

"It was all the parts from that part number used in their afternoon shift," he said.

"Have you or any of your people been over to the plant to investigate? Did you check their vehicles or gauges?" I said.

"No, not yet," he responded.

"I want you and several of your people to get down to that Global Motors plant right away, determine the extent that our parts are out of spec, on which shift, and then take measurements of our parts and the vehicle parts that the wheels are going onto. Then try to determine exactly what the problem is and whose fault it is. At the same time, have some of your people check our equipment and gauges here on our production line, and I also want you to 100 percent inspect every part of that type that comes off our line before any more of these parts are shipped. Take care of this immediately this morning, and let them know that we will do everything to make this right, OK?" I said.

"I will do that right away," he responded as he ran out of my office.

****

Katey walked in at exactly eleven o'clock, and George came in just a moment later.

"Have a seat at the conference table. We have much to discuss," I told them. "I hope you got some rest last night because there are a number of things I want to talk to you about. Before I begin, though, I want to thank both of you for the fantastic job you did with regard to our trip, arranging things, finding existing and potential vendors, working with the FBI, and so much more. I may not have mentioned too much while we were there, but I noticed everything that you both did and I really appreciate all your hard work."

They both smiled and nodded to show their appreciation of my comments.

"Now, first, we have some issues with one of our part numbers. I spoke with Billy this morning, and he and a few of his people should already be on their way down to the Global Motors plant to deal with the issue. Some of our parts appear to be out of spec, and we have been put on containment. He will bring us up to date after he returns from the plant. We have to address this issue immediately to minimize the costs associated with our containment status, as well as show our customer that we are on top of the issue and have taken care of the underlying causes."

I knew George and Katey understood what containment status was, how expensive it could become, and how important it was to get us removed from this status as soon as possible.

"Next, I believe we have several other things we also need to deal with immediately. Please feel free to break in with your thoughts whenever you want. I am depending on both of you to help me move things forward. Katey, I want to verify as quickly as possible the new vendors we found on our trip. We need to make sure that they can get us parts of the right quality and quantity at the right cost, based on our needs. We will need to get production samples of the parts we discussed with each of them as soon as possible and then lead times on production volumes."

Next, we need to make sure that we lose as few of our existing customers as possible due to the price changes that will most likely be coming, and then begin finding new customers for these parts. George, I will need you to determine what our actual costs will be and then we can determine a new sales price for our customers. Hopefully, although we were selling stolen parts obviously acquired at a very low cost, most of those potential profits were siphoned off by Cal, Herb, and Marty, and the sales price may have been high enough that we will not have to raise prices too much. I will need you to work on that and get back to us as quickly as possible. Next, George, I want you to see if you can begin sourcing the same parts domestically, preferably in this general geographic area. That is Ohio, Wisconsin, Indiana, Michigan, and Illinois for example. The proximity and shipping savings may make them more attractive than we had anticipated. Then, as we look longer-term, I want you to check with our engineers to see if we can begin making some of these parts ourselves, possibly even after purchasing some used equipment. I have done some preliminary checking, and it appears that at least a few of our high-volume customers use exactly the same wheels, for example, for many vehicles with only the hole configuration being different. I am hoping that we can purchase the wheels in volume, then drill the holes ourselves with automated equipment. Then we would benefit from the volume savings and obtain additional overhead from that process as well. What do you think?

George told me he knew some reliable used equipment dealers that he had dealt with in the past and would contact them as soon as he had the specs and had spoken with our engineers.

Then Katey said, "I will begin making some courtesy calls to our customers just to give them a general, high-level view of what has been going on. I'll only mention that we are re-sourcing our products to improve quality and service, and I will get back to them to let them know if there will be any potential price changes, either up or down."

"Good idea, Katey," I said.

"George, your knowledge of the equipment dealer community will be invaluable in determining if these ideas are viable. Also, as soon as you have the numbers, we will all discuss them and determine which direction to go. Next, I want to begin planning out together a long-term strategy to put this company on a proper footing, stabilize our customer base, increase volumes and overhead absorption, and begin expanding our product base with new products, hopefully ones where we can do a value add to increase profitability. We will speak about this after we have jumped over these immediate hurdles. Sound good? Any questions or comments?"

George was the first to respond. "As soon as I get the exact costs from our new vendors, I will add shipping costs and other expenses and determine our total unit cost, and then we can discuss a reasonable selling price. I hope to have all of that within the next week or two, at most. I will also start looking to see if we can source some of these parts domestically, preferably, as you suggested, in our general geographic area, and then determine what those costs will be for comparison. Finally, I will also begin working on additional products that we can produce on a value-added basis."

I then interrupted. "Katey, can you start feeling out some of our customers to see what their needs are for associated parts that they may be having some problems with in terms of quality, service, or price from their current suppliers, or that you feel, just from general conversations with current and prospective customers, are the kinds of products we should be looking at? Then you, George, and I can spend more time exploring this area for expansion and refinement."

Katey and George agreed.

"You know," I said, "We have a finite amount of time to accomplish all of this. The judge was very clear as to how long Herb and Marty are to stay disassociated from this company. We need to use that time wisely to bring financial stability to the company. We owe it to our employees, our customers, and our lending institutions. If and when Herb and Marty are allowed to return, I do not plan to remain here. I don't know if either of you do, but that is our upper time limit right now."

Both George and Katey acknowledged they understood the gravity of the situation and the time constraints we were under. They also agreed that this would not be an assignment they would like to retain after Herb and Marty returned.

"Oh, George, can you also arrange to have our bank representatives and CPA firm come in to meet with us, preferably our CPA firm first and then the bank to explain to our loan officers exactly what has transpired, where we are now, and what we plan to do about it, as well as what our financial needs will be? I think we need to be very upfront with all of them to regain their trust and make sure we have their support going forward."

"No problem. I will get on that right away as well," he said.

"Thanks. I really appreciate your quick responses," I concluded.

In the early afternoon, I received a call from Billy. "We are still down here at Global and found some interesting things. First, I heard from our guys that stayed at our plant. They have certified every gauge and verified that all the associated production equipment is well within spec, and rechecked all of the incoming inspection documentation. Everything at our plant is fine. Next, it appears the problem with our wheels only occurs on their afternoon shift. We just finished speaking with the day shift maintenance supervisor and afternoon shift maintenance supervisor, as you suggested, and found that the problem was happening only on the later shift. Then, as you also suggested, we had each one of those maintenance supervisors show us how they set the tolerances for the equipment at the beginning of each shift. Sure enough, the day shift supervisor set them within the proper tolerance limits, but the afternoon shift supervisor set them differently, outside the predetermined tolerances, because he felt that was the best way. As a result, their parts—not ours—were being ground incorrectly, and therefore our parts did fit into their parts on their day shift operation, but not during their afternoon shift operation. Although they did finally admit that we were right, there was no apology from anyone."

"Great job, Billy. Please make certain that before you leave, you have them move us off containment immediately. That is very important!" I told him.

"I will go right to our buyer and their chief engineer to have them take care of that," Billy answered.

After this episode, we all got very busy with day-to-day operations, trying to stabilize and grow the company and correct all that had gone on in previous years, and at the same time, plan for the future. George had arranged for our meeting with our CPAs and attorneys, and for another meeting immediately afterward, at which our bankers would join all of us in my office conference room.

Early Tuesday morning, barely a week after we had returned from our trip, Amy rang my office to let me know that it was nine o'clock, and that our outside accountants and our attorneys were in the lobby. I told her to send them all in, and to have George and Katey come in as well.

As they came in, I greeted them. "Hi, Bill. Hi, Andrew. Good to see you. Hi, Mitch and Dave. How are you doing? Have a seat. George and Katey will be right in. How have you been?"

"We are fine, and I am sure all of us are very interested to hear about your trip and about your plans going forward," Bill said.

"Well, the trip was very educational and, I believe, successful, but we have much more work to do in a number of areas. As you also know, our bankers will be in to see all of us right after our meeting here," I added.

"Great," Andrew said. "I look forward to speaking with them, but of course, after hearing from you first how you plan to get things going again the right way and what your plans are for the future."

There was a knock at the door, and George and Katey came in. They shook hands with Bill and Andrew, and Mitch and Dave, and exchanged greetings.

"Well, let me give you a very brief overview of our trip, and then we can get down to work. We visited India, China, and Taiwan. We learned a lot about some of our existing suppliers and some potential new ones. A number of them were heavily involved in selling stolen merchandise to us and, in fact, the local authorities were brought in as well as the FBI agents who had come along with us to deal with these companies. At the same time, we found some potential new suppliers that actually have manufacturing capacity to make the parts that we need. George has the pricing on these parts and has calculated how our costs and potential sales prices would compare to what our company has been selling the stolen merchandise for. He will speak to you about that in a few minutes. Also, George has been trying to source some of these parts domestically from our general geographic area, in some of the surrounding states. He will also speak to you about that. We, of course, will need your help to determine the viability of these plans, as well as for some of our plans going forward, but we can wait a few minutes for that discussion. George, why don't you go ahead with your findings? After that, I want Katey to discuss what she has found out about our current and potential customers with regard to new suppliers and pricing and potential new products. George, why don't you start?" I said.

George described the new suppliers and provided comparisons between costs and sales prices for our existing line of products, particularly the ones we had imported from the companies that were selling us stolen merchandise.

"In summary," George concluded, "I believe we can sell legitimately manufactured parts imported from these new suppliers at only a slightly higher sales price than we had been doing in the past, and at a reasonable profitability level as well. In addition, I have located a few domestically based suppliers that we can begin switching some of our sourcing to. Along with a reduction in shipping costs, quality costs, and close proximity, there would be little impact on our bottom line. Finally, after Katey tells about her findings, we believe we can begin manufacturing some of these outsourced products and also manufacture new products that will provide us with additional volume and overhead absorption, and much better margins than some of our existing product lines," George said.

Bill and Andrew indicated that they were impressed and, at an initial cursory level, agreed with George's presentation.

Then Katey began. "I have been speaking with a number of our larger existing customers and some potential new customers. I have been accumulating data about some of the products they might want us to provide them, ones where they were having problems with their existing suppliers, wanted to outsource from their own manufacturing processes, or were looking to bring down some of their costs. Fortunately, our overhead rates are significantly lower than theirs as they have a good deal of legacy costs, very high wage rates and benefit costs, and much less efficient operations and processes than we do. These sheets explain my findings," Katey concluded, passing out the printed materials that she had prepared.

While Bill and Andrew were also impressed with Katey's data and conclusions, they indicated that they still wanted to review them in more detail.

"Now, finally, before we meet with our bankers, we have some associated issues to discuss. "First," I said, "we need to lay this all out for the bankers in a positive light, so they will continue to finance us during this rebuild phase. Next, we need to convince them that they should support our ongoing and increased capital needs, so that we can finance the additional inventory, support our accounts receivable during this period and, most importantly, provide for our capital needs to purchase the additional equipment needed to begin producing some of the new parts George and Katey have been speaking about. Do you think you can make a convincing argument to them now?" I asked.

Everyone nodded in agreement.

"Also, Mitch and Dave, we will need both of you to chime in with regard to the legal status of Marty, Herb, and Cal; our success in obtaining a good part of the money the three of them had illegally sent to the Cayman Bank; and most importantly, the legality of what we are doing here now in their absence. That's just in case the bankers are concerned that any of Herb's kids, the old CPAs or attorneys, or any of their accomplices are going to be returning anytime soon. I want the bankers to have a very clear picture of the situation and sufficient comfort level to continue providing us with financing. Does that all make sense?"

All agreed in unison.

I called Amy to ask if the new bankers had arrived. She said they had just come in, and I asked her to send them in. Fred Jackson, senior lender and vice president of midmarket lending at First National Bank of Illinois, had been in the banking business for over thirty years and knew just about all there was to know about commercial lending. He was a tall and muscular man, with a rugged face and a deep voice, and he came in with his junior lending officer, Pam Cannon. Pam was attractive, of average height but slim, and, in her upper thirties, a good deal younger than Fred. She was also very knowledgeable about banking practices. I introduced them to all present, and we all exchanged pleasantries and business cards.

I said, "I want to welcome all of you here this morning, and we want you all to know how much we appreciate you coming in. We have a good deal of ground to cover, so I will start by describing briefly what has transpired here at SMI in the past several months. Then I will have George Montry, our CFO, and Katey Sommers, our director of sales, speak. Then you will hear from representatives of our new outside CPA firm and, finally, from our new attorneys. We want you to be fully aware of what is going on with the company, and what our plans are for the future. We want to make you a part of our growth.

"As you may know, a number of months ago we found that several individuals here at the company had been involved in purchasing stolen merchandise for sale, skimming money from those sales, hiding that money in the Cayman Islands, and more. By court order, they have been removed from the company and are not allowed to have any contact with the company during the next five years, at a minimum. The IRS and criminal court system will be dealing with them during that time. We have recovered a good deal of the funds that were stolen from the company and used those monies to hire the new people you see here today. In addition, we have paid off some of the debt that was incurred as a result of these illegal actions. We have hired George and Katey to assume positions on the management team, and they have done an exceptional job already. To avoid any additional impropriety or even a hint of that, we have replaced our outside accounting and legal firms with the representatives you see sitting here today, and they are already taking an active part in the rebuilding of this company on an ethical basis and helping the company move forward and grow. Now I want you to hear from George and Katey about what they have been doing and what their plans are for the company."

George explained all that had gone on with Herb, Marty, and Cal, including the FBI's involvement; what we were doing in terms of re-sourcing; and our plans for additional in-house manufacturing. Katey then talked about our trip to India, China, and Taiwan, the legitimate and dishonest companies we visited, her discussions with current and prospective customers, our potential new products, and general sales estimates. Bill and Andrew discussed the current financial status of the company and projected profit-and-loss and balance sheet estimates for this year and coming years based on the expansion of products and manufacturing we had planned. Mitch and Dave discussed the legal ramifications of what Herb, Marty, and Cal had been involved in, and any potential impact on the company and our operations.

Finally, I spoke to our bankers, Fred and Pam.

"Well, Fred and Pam, you have heard all that has gone on and what our intentions are. We have tried to be very upfront with you and present the good and bad as to what has transpired these past several months. What do you think about what you have heard? Do you have any problems with continuing to support our operation and providing us with additional lending capacity for our planned expansion of product and manufacturing?"

There was a pause that seemed to go on forever, but was probably just fifteen to twenty seconds, then Fred spoke.

"Well, I have to tell you all that I am very impressed with your presentations and with how you have responded to a very ugly situation and how much you have accomplished in such a short time. Having said that, I have to tell you I am obviously very concerned about how the company got into this mess, and what impact that entire situation will have on the short-term and long-term viability of the company. We, the bank, certainly need to protect our investment, as you can well understand. While your projections look reasonable and viable, they are only projections, and our loan committee and I need to be concerned about whether your projections will come to fruition, how you will protect your assets and cash flow, and how well you will be able to service the current and future debt going forward. We will take all this back to the office, and our loan committee will review this, as will our analysts, so that we can respond to you."

"Fred," I asked, "what is your gut feeling? Can you—no, *will* you—continue financing our recovery and expansion? I need to know as soon as possible because we fully intend to make this all happen, but if your bank will not be able to assist us, then we will need to go look elsewhere—and very quickly," I said.

Fred and Pam seemed a little stunned by my comments. They stared at each other for a moment, and then Fred responded.

"Well, let's not do anything rash. As I said, we will be reviewing all this material and all of your comments and will make a determination, so there is no need for you to go to another financial institution. I will put a rush on this review, and we should have a response to you within a week. Does that sound reasonable?"

"That's fine, but I cannot emphasize enough the amount of time and effort we have already put in, and continue to spend in order to make and keep this company viable. Everyone sitting at this table has a vested interest in making this all work, one way or another, so we need a quick response and a positive one as well," I answered.

Fred and Pam reiterated that they would get back to us shortly, said their goodbyes, and exited the room. Then Bill, Andrew, Mitch, and Dave did as well.

I looked at George and Katey, and said, "Let's go to lunch."

As we prepared to leave, both Amy and April called within a few minutes of each other to tell me that they had received phone calls asking for Herb or Marty or Cal. More importantly, when they told the callers the person they had asked for was not associated with the company at this time and asked if anyone else could help, the callers got nasty and hung up. I thought nothing of it at the time, but calls of this type became more frequent. They involved several callers and were increasingly intrusive and nasty. After a week or two, I decided to contact Agent

Andersen. I described what was happening, and he felt it warranted a visit. That was on a Wednesday.

Agent Andersen arrived on Thursday, and after I explained what was going on, he told me how he wanted to approach it.

"We are very fortunate to have just received some brand-new equipment for this sort of thing in the Chicago office. In fact, we are the first FBI office in the country to have this new equipment. Let me explain how it works. First, we put this small button on your phones with incoming lines. With this system, we can now trace calls in ten seconds or less, and we can even locate cell phones at their precise location and address. Because we will be able to immediately identify the owner of the phone and the location, we will potentially know why they are doing this. The minute any of your people answers the phone and identifies that this is one of these types of calls, they only have to push this button and our electronic equipment will be activated automatically. Afterward, our programs will identify the call and assess its frequency relative to the prior similar calls. Then we, at the same time as you, will receive an instant report displayed on our computers, showing a summary of the calls, point of origination, and the name of the caller. The report will also identify if a burner cell phone is being used, and it can even recognize voice patterns to help identify the caller, along with a summary of all similar calls. There is also additional automatic analysis that will come along with this data. After a period of time, we can discuss what is happening and what to do about it. Does that sound reasonable?"

I agreed, and he went to the two incoming phone locations, installed the buttons, and explained to the receptionists what to do.

Agent Andersen told me I would get an email each time the caller report was updated. I thanked him and he left. Although I was apprehensive about the results, I was certain we would have data in a short period of time. I just wasn't sure what the data would show. It didn't take long to start getting results. The calls were coming in and were being identified. I checked my computer and found the email from Agent Andersen. The associated report showed most of the calls came from several different numbers, but with just a few owners and locations. There were a few random, probably legitimate calls, but the bulk came from four identified people. Two attorneys associated with SMI's old law firm generated the bulk of the calls. Next came phones and locations associated with Herb and Marty.

We left the trace equipment on for about two weeks. I then called Agent Andersen in to discuss the findings: I invited Mitch Conner to be present as well. The results spoke for themselves. The calls were being made by or for Marty and Herb to harass and intimidate us.

Agent Andersen was the first to speak. "You have all seen the results of just two weeks of calls, where they are coming from, and who is involved.

The big question is 'What do you want to do about it, if anything?'" he asked.

I said, "I would like your opinion with regard to what the FBI position is on these kinds of matters and your recommendation. Then we can hear from Mitch, our attorney."

"I believe they are violating laws, and while these actions have not crossed state lines, they are using public communications services, and the individuals are already involved with the IRS and criminal justice system for what they have done until now. I would have no problem pursuing this out of our office, but you might want to take an approach from your company, at least initially," he said.

Then Mitch spoke. "Personally, I believe we should send letters to Herb, Marty, and their legal counsel indicating that we are aware of what they are doing, that we have identified them as the callers, and that what they are doing is illegal harassment and intimidation. We can also remind them that unless they cease and desist these actions immediately, we will forward this information to the presiding judge to evaluate for further criminal action. I think that should get their attention."

"I agree," I said. "What do you think, Agent Andersen?"

"Yes, I believe that is a good first step. Why don't you do that and see the results? We can always move to the next step and get involved out of our office," he said.

"Mitch, can you prepare the letters and send them out after I review them? You might want to add that although the judge ordered them to have no association with the company for a fixed period of time, that period could easily be extended, potentially indefinitely, if their illegal actions continue and we make that information available directly to the judge. Let's nip this in the bud before it gets worse. Thanks."

Since we had all decided to leave the tracing equipment on longer that the original two weeks, the email messages and reports kept coming to my computer as the calls continued, and two days later, the letters went out from our attorney. Several days later, the calls abruptly ended and did not begin again.

George, Katey, and I decided it was time to bring our employees into the loop, let them understand what was going on, and let them be part of the solution. I asked George to schedule a companywide meeting for the coming Friday during break time. I prepared myself with all of the facts, and at ten thirty Friday morning, I went out into the plant. The break-time buzzer rang, and with my portable microphone, I called everyone in the office and plant to gather around me.

I began: "I am sure many of you are aware that a number of things have been going on here, and I want to bring everyone up to date with what has happened, what we are doing about it, and what the future may bring. A few months ago, it was determined that a few people running the company, Herb Henderson, Marty Gilbert, and Cal Donaven, were alleged to have been involved in the purchase and distribution of stolen goods. I am not saying any more about this because the entire matter is currently under investigation and in the control of the Internal Revenue Service and the criminal justice system. What I can tell you is that a judge has ruled that these three individuals are to be removed from the company for a specified period of time, and that they were to have no contact with the company at all during that time, which is currently set at five years. The judge also ruled at the time that I would be put in charge of the company for at least that interval of time specified, the five years, to try to correct any impact on the company, and to move the company forward in an honest, straightforward fashion in order to keep the company open and operating, and to retain all of your jobs. I have done that with a number of changes, which I want to outline for you right now.

"First, I hired George Montry, standing here next to me on my right, as the new CFO of the company. I also hired Katherine—we call her Katey—Sommers, standing next to me on my left, as the new director of sales. Next, to prevent any suggestion of impropriety, I replaced our existing outside accounting firm and outside legal firm with new ones that I know, trust, and have had thoroughly checked out. This team has assisted me thus far in correcting many of the problems the company has had, and in planning for the future. Now, I am sure the biggest question on your minds is what is going to happen to you and to your jobs. While I cannot predict the future, at this point we feel good about the new vendors we have secured to replace the unethical ones that were apparently involved in the sale and distribution of stolen property. Next we are investigating the possibility of new domestic suppliers of equal or better quality. We have also had many conversations with our bankers and are in the process of securing new and expanded financing, so we can move the company forward. Finally, we are looking at expanding our product offerings to bring more work and sales into the company to make all of our jobs even more secure.

"Now, you should know that there are currently no plans, I repeat, no plans to lay off or fire anyone. If anything, we plan to hire additional employees as time goes on and our sales improve. You should also know that this is not just the job of George, Katey, the office staff, or me. This also involves every single one of you working to make the company and our jobs secure. This means reducing scrap, working as efficiently as possible, coming in on time every day, making quality parts, and even improving quality where possible. If customers are happy with us, they will purchase more product and we will all have jobs. If they are not happy with us, in any way, we will lose sales and lose our jobs. It is as simple as that. If you have a suggestion as to how we can be more efficient and productive, and thereby successful, please let me, George, or Katey know what your idea is. We will appreciate it, and, if we are able to implement those ideas, it will help make all of our jobs more secure. We plan on growing this company in the future, but we need every single person here to help do that. I am depending on all of you for the success of this company. In a few weeks, I plan to have another similar meeting to provide you with some hard data as to where we are, and to be able to answer any questions you might have. Thank you."

I watched everyone walk away and go back to work, looking carefully at their faces. They appeared to be satisfied with what I had said, although still nervous about what had happened and wondering if I could do everything I had told them I would. A few employees even came up to thank me for what I had said and for what we were doing to allow the company to continue to stay in business and to grow.

One employee, Wesley Johnson, told me he had thought something was wrong because he had seen so many boxes of parts coming from overseas and simply being repackaged with no work done on them. He said he was happy to hear that not only had we found new vendors but that we would be finding new domestic sources as well. I thanked him for all his hard work and told him I looked forward to his continued employment and support.

The following Monday morning, I received a call from Fred. He told me he would stop by the next day to bring our new loan agreements. We had been approved for new lines of credit and an increase in our loan capacity to support increased inventory, accounts receivable, and capital expenditures relative to our plans for new products and additional manufacturing capacity. He also told me that we would be subject to a monthly reporting requirement for at least one year, and then, based on our performance and our ability to meet our goals, that would be changed to a six-month reporting period, and then, hopefully, to an annual one.

At nine thirty the next morning, Tuesday, April called to let me know that Fred was waiting for me. I told her to bring him in and asked her to call George and Katey to come in as well. They came in a few moments later, and Fred began.

"I met with our loan committee, presented them all the information you had discussed with Pam and me the last time I was in, as well as your comments about possibly seeking a relationship with a new bank. They approved an increase in your line of credit to five million dollars, and an additional three million for capital expenditures that would be rolled over to a demand note, once you have finished purchasing your new equipment. The line and notes will be secured with accounts receivable at sixty percent based on sixty days, inventory at forty percent, and fixed assets and equipment at ninety percent of appraisal. Along with this, as we previously discussed, we will need you to go on a monthly reporting schedule for accounts receivable, inventory, accounts payable, and cash balance. How does that sound?"

George began, "First, the percentages you are using are really unacceptably low and would be essentially impossible to work with. On accounts receivable we would need a minimum of ninety days at eighty percent, and inventory of a minimum of fifty percent."

"Fred," I began, "what George just said is completely correct, and I have a problem with monthly reporting requirements that are open-ended. Why don't you use six months and if we meet all our requirements and remain within our covenants, we can move automatically to an annual reporting schedule the following year?" I asked.

Katey then said, "As we explained with our presentation when you were in last, it would take a while to ramp up new sales for existing products with the new vendors, and longer for new products."

She said she was already making progress identifying potential new products, estimated volumes, profitability, and costs.

Fred was quiet for a moment, deep in thought, and then he responded. "OK, we will go with your requests and change the things you mentioned, and do monthly reporting for just an initial six-month period. I will have new loan documents prepared and send them over to you to sign and return. I knew you were tough negotiators, but I feel this will help you and us in the long run as you grow the business. Anything else?"

"Well," I said, "actually there is. We need to reduce the interest rate on the line of credit if this is going to work. It is at least one and one-half points too high. We need to get that dropped as well. We need to survive and grow, and we just can't do that under your restrictions. Remember, our success is your success."

"You guys are tough!" he quipped. "As I said, I will get everything else changed, and will speak to the committee to see what I can do with the interest rate. I will call you no later than tomorrow morning."

"Thanks, Fred. I appreciate it. You know we want to stay with your bank and have you grow with us, but we really need this all to work for both of us," I said.

"OK, I will do my best," Fred responded and left.

At nine o'clock the next morning, Fred called to say he had gotten approval for all the changes we requested and would overnight the loan documents to us. We needed to sign and return them as soon as possible.

The following morning we received the documents. I sent a copy to Mitch, who reviewed them and gave me the OK, and I signed them all and sent them right back to Fred.

At least the banking had been put in place for now, and we could begin working on the rest of our plans. All of us were very busy, and time passed quickly. I established a weekly meeting with George and Katey for us to share ideas, problems, updates, and so on. We agreed that nine o'clock on Friday mornings would be a good time to have these meetings, either in person or by phone depending on where each of us was at that time.

While they were pretty similar each week, following a fairly consistent format, one that occurred several weeks later was a little unusual.

"Good morning, Katey. Good morning, George," I said.

"How are you doing? I have much to tell you, so I can't wait to get started," Katey said.

Well, let's do that right now. Have a seat here at the table," I said. "Katey, why don't you begin today?"

"Well, first I want to tell both of you that we are getting a lot of traction with our new and existing customers in terms of additional sales, after I explained to each of them what had happened this past year and what we are doing about it. Virtually every single customer is very impressed with how we are approaching the situation, the new vendors we have found, and our vetting process. In addition, quite a number of customers, both aftermarket and OEM, have provided me, at my request, with lists of parts that they would like to source to us, at the right price, of course. I have consolidated the lists from all the customers and have come up with ten potential parts for us to produce. I have been working with George to determine our costs; whether we need to purchase them from outside or if we can manufacture them ourselves; if there is substantial value-add potential; if we need to source components, and if so, if we can source them domestically, possibly from surrounding states or even locally. The answers to these criteria have been mostly positive, and George and I believe we have some real opportunities available to us, and at a relatively low entry cost."

"Thanks, Katey. That all sounds great," I responded. "Please provide me with a spreadsheet summary listing of all the potential new products, estimated entry cost, margins per unit, estimated volumes, and names of customers that have already expressed concrete interest. George, of course, I will want you to continue working with Katey on the cost side of these products as well as equipment costs, installation costs, and those kinds of things. What do you have to report, George?" I asked.

"Well, most of what I would want to speak about, Katey just covered. Another item is that our cash flow is good, and we are using our line of credit to purchase inventory and support accounts-receivable growth. What I am very gratified to find is that we are profitable even though we switched over to several of our new vendors for those components that were previously involved in the stolen goods arena. Katey and I have also found a few domestic suppliers for existing products that should prove more profitable than our current overseas suppliers, and we intend to get them on stream as soon as possible. We'll start with just the excess volumes until we determine how well they can supply us quality parts, on time, at their quoted costs," George said.

Katey interjected. "There is one more thing I want to speak about, and it is of great concern to me, and I need assistance from both of you to sort this out.

"A few weeks ago, I received a call from a potential aftermarket customer. The name of the company is Tennessee Automotive, and they are located near Memphis. The gentlemen who called me gave his name as Robert Perry, and he said he had heard we were considering manufacturing a few parts that he would like to purchase. He indicated that he was particularly interested in an underbody bracket and said he would like to order twelve thousand initially and then to place orders in twenty-five thousand increments. I questioned him as to where he heard of our plans, and he said he didn't remember and that it was probably in discussions with some friends who were also in the automotive business. It just didn't seem right, so I immediately checked on the company and Mr. Perry, and both checked out OK. The company is a long-established aftermarket supplier. Mr. Perry has been owner, president and CEO for a number of years. I could not find any hole in the story, but it still didn't seem right," she said.

I responded, "Katey, I trust your judgment, and I think we should dig a little deeper, particularly since we have not even made the decision to go ahead and manufacture these parts. George, why don't you check with some of your old contacts and get a good private investigator to check into this guy and his affiliations, banking connections, friends, and other automotive contacts to see how they fit in. Also check with our attorneys to see if they can get a handle on this company and Mr. Perry. Have our people check to see if there is any connection to Herb, Marty, or Cal personally, or to their legal or accounting people. Katey, I agree, this does not smell right to me either."

It didn't take long to get answers from George's contacts, our private investigator, and our attorneys. Within a week, answers were coming in, and they were not pretty. Yes, Mr. Perry had connections to Herb and Marty. Yes, he was an old friend of Herb's who had, at one time, belonged to the same country club, and, yes, they had been in contact recently. Yes, Marty had also met with Mr. Perry some time ago, he had also had been in contact with Mr. Perry recently.

I was confident that we could deal with this issue through a restraining order from the court and an appropriately worded letter to Mr. Perry. I had greater concern about what happened shortly thereafter.

Chapter 10

Scary and More

Not even a week later, my phone rang; it was Amy telling me there were three foreign-speaking gentlemen in the lobby asking to see me regarding a business deal. Although I was busy and certainly did not have much time for an unannounced visit, I told her to send them in and to ask George and Katey to join us. Three large men came in, all dressed in black suits, shirts, and ties. The first introduced himself as Dimitri Petrovich from Russia and the other two as his associates.

"Good morning. My name ees Dimitri Petrovich," he said in a very heavy Russian accent. "And theese are my associates. I am the president of Russian Automotive Group, and we are here visiting some companies that we have identified as good partners for our automotive beesiniss."

His associates just stood silently.

"Mr. Petrovich," I began, "I appreciate your visit, but I really don't have much time today, and honestly, we are not looking for any partners right now."

"That ees unimportant; we still want to be your partner," he said.

"I repeat, we are not looking for any partners right now. We have just gone through a difficult time and are in the midst of getting our business back on track. While I appreciate your suggestion, this really is not the right time for us to be considering any such offer," I responded.

"Again, we still want to be your partner and we will do whatever it takes to do so. We will be back in two weeks to finalize our deal. By the way, do you chove any family in Russia?" he asked.

"What do you mean?" I countered.

"Do you chove any family or friends now living in Russia who might be at risk? You know, things can happen at any time," he said.

Although I didn't have any family in Russia, his attitude and words concerned me. I tried to close the conversation as quickly as possible.

"Again, we do not want to create a partnership at this time, but I appreciate your coming in today."

"I will be back in two weeks to conclude our deal," Dimitri said, as he and his two associates left my office and the building. George and Katey stood with mouths open in shock and amazement, as I'm sure, I did. We just stood there for a minute or so, not knowing what to say.

"Well, I really do not like the sound of that conversation. I took it as a direct threat to me and the company. What do you think?" I asked.

"I was scared stiff by these guys and what Dimitri said. I don't think they were here to be our partners," Katey chimed in.

"I believe this guy and his two goons just want to take over the company by any and all means possible, and I don't think he will stop at anything to accomplish his goals. This was not a discussion or a negotiation. He was stating facts," George said.

"I am going to contact Agent Andersen at the FBI. I believe we will need at least his help, and possibly other governmental agencies such as Homeland Security and maybe even the CIA. I really didn't like the sound of this conversation. I am going to call him right now. Why don't you two stick around? I will put him on speakerphone," I said.

I dialed Agent Andersen on his cell phone and he answered. George, Katey, and I explained what had happened, and he simply said, "Wait there. I will be there in an hour."

Just under an hour later he entered my office, where we were waiting.

"You really hit the jackpot with this one," Agent Andersen began. "Dimitri Petrovich is the front man for a large Russian mafia organization, located in Moscow, but expanding into many countries. This, as you described it, fits his pattern of so-called partnerships, where he literally takes over companies, initially as a partner; pushes out the existing owners; and then uses the company to launder Russian mafia money into U.S. dollars. They have no hesitation about using intimidation, threats, assaults, arson, and even, in some instances, murder. I am very glad you contacted me immediately because if we are to do anything about this, we have to act quickly."

"Well, I've got to tell you, I have a very bad feeling in the pit of my stomach, and, yes, I am frightened and nervous about what he might do. And, yes, I am intimidated," I said.

"That's OK and understandable. It may help ease your mind if we begin implementing a plan to not only catch him and his thugs but put an end to his intimidation, if you are willing to go ahead with my plan. I would like to have you help us catch these guys and put them away for a long, long time," Agent Andersen said.

"Why don't you tell us what you have in mind before we tell you if we are willing to go along with your plan?" I said.

Agent Anderson said, "He told you he would be back in two weeks, right?"

"That's correct," I responded.

"Here's what I want you to do. Have the meeting with Dimitri and his men in two weeks here in your office. I will want you to wear a wire, which is a listening device connected to a recording device. We will also install hidden microphones and video cameras in the walls and ceilings to make sure we capture the entire conversation digitally so that we will have our evidence. Also, just to be safe, I will have all three of you wear lightweight bulletproof vests under your clothing. The new ones that we have available are not even visible under your clothing. We will have people working here in various capacities every day as backup. They will be dressed as electricians, plumbers, phone repair people, technology repair people, and similar types of professionals so as not to draw suspicion, but to be available as backup."

I nodded. "Sounds like you have covered a number of bases, but I would really like some added levels of comfort, if you don't mind. Hopefully, you have some additional suggestions, but I would like one or two additional things. First, can you please do a thorough background check on our last six months of hires, just to make sure they are not plants in any way? Also, please make sure that you or other agents use not only unmarked vehicles, but make sure they look like standard cars, not government vehicles. I am really concerned about Dimitri and his people, and I don't want any hint that government agencies are involved. Finally, I think we need to thoroughly discuss this plan, rehearse it, and make sure everyone is on the same page while keeping this completely confidential among us," I continued. "To be brutally honest, I—I mean we—are petrified about this entire situation."

"Makes sense to me. That was our plan anyway," said Agent Andersen.

"I do want you to know I plan to add in a few additional levels of security. We will be making some minor alterations to your facilities. This will accomplish two things. First, it will provide a reason for other agents to be on the premises, getting the lay of the land, so to speak, and watching current employees, vendors, and the like. Second, it will provide better access for our people should that be needed on an instantaneous basis. Most important, we will be adding a few access points to your office and conference room, in addition to appropriate surveillance provisions. We will be doing some of the work during the day, and some late at night. Is that all OK with you?"

"Absolutely," I responded.

Work progressed for the next two weeks, and I tried to keep tabs on what was being done. At the same time, Agent Andersen and Agent Parker were keeping me up to date on their investigation of Petrovich, his accomplices, organization, and employers. The time passed quickly. George, Katey, and I were fitted with lightweight Kevlar-type bulletproof vests. This way we would have an additional level of protection that would not be obvious to anyone who saw us.

To say that I was nervous would be an understatement. I was petrified, but it was something that had to be done. Agent Andersen had assured us many times that this operation would be made as safe as possible for everyone involved and that we would be fully protected and under surveillance at all times.

All those assurances just weren't enough for me to relax. My stomach spent a good deal of time in my throat, and I was shaking like a leaf inside. I don't believe I have ever been so nervous and afraid.

Finally the planned meeting day arrived, but to our surprise, I received a call from April on the intercom, saying that a woman who was associated with Petrovich was in the lobby and asking if she could send her in. I told her to do so. A knockout beautiful young woman with the body of a beauty queen walked into my office. She had long blond hair, a very tight blouse, a tight short skirt, and very high heels, and she appeared to be about thirty to thirty-five years old.

She began before I could even welcome her. "My name is Galina Ikanov," she said in flawless English with virtually no Russian accent. "I work with Dimitri Petrovich, and he asked me to come to let you know he is running a little late and will be here in about thirty minutes. He asked me to begin our negotiations with regard to our new partnership with you."

"It is very nice to meet you, Miss Ikanov, but as I told Mr. Petrovich a few weeks ago, there are no negotiations and there is no partnership," I said.

She chose to not even hear me and continued. "We will need a current P&L and balance sheet; list of current employees, customers and vendors; a breakdown of your costing structure; and a number of other things. When can you have these all ready for me to review?" she demanded.

"As I said, Miss Ikanov, I will not be providing these documents to you, and there is no partnership negotiation. I really don't know how much clearer I can make this," I said.

She appeared frustrated, and she got on her cell phone and spoke softly to someone in what sounded like Russian. In the meantime, I called George and Katey and asked them to come in to my office. As she got off her cell phone, George and Katey came in, and I introduced them to her. As they spoke briefly, Amy called me on the intercom to let me know that Dimitri and his people were there and waiting to come in.

I told her to send them in, and an almost uncontrollable shaking started inside me. I took a sip of water from the glass on my desk and waited for the door to open and Dimitri to walk in.

He did, along with the same two goons he had brought last time.

"Mister Kirby, good to see you again. I see you have met my assistant, Miss Ikanov. She tells me that there is some misunderstanding with regard to our partnership negotiations. What is the problem?" he began.

"Mr. Petrovich," I said, "there is no problem and no misunderstanding. As I explained to you the last time you were here and to Miss Ikanov today, we have had a very difficult time the past several months and we have dealt with a number of very serious issues. The company is just beginning to return to normalcy now, and the last thing on our minds is any sort of partnership. I do not know where you got the idea that we wanted such an arrangement right now, but we do not."

"Mister Kirby," he continued, "it is not a matter of what you want right now; there will be a partnership, including you or not. This is going to happen. Now, whether you will be around to see it or not is your decision. I can only tell you that my associates have helped me with situations like this in the past and, in some cases, the executives at the company we chose to partner with have survived, and in some cases, they did not, rest their souls, and they were eliminated. Now can we proceed?"

"Mr. Petrovich, that sounds like a threat to me and my staff."

"No, it is not a threat, but rather a promise of what will happen if you choose not to cooperate. We chove had this happen before with unwilling partners, and we have dealt with them accordingly. Some are now at the bottom of the sea, buried in construction projects, or have had unfortunate accidents falling off buildings. I assume you do not want to end up like any of them. Am I right?"

"I certainly don't, but I don't think I can go ahead with your partnership plans either," I said.

Suddenly, shiny objects came out from under Dimitri's and his goon's jackets, and guns were definitely pointed at me. I froze. It took what seemed like an eternity, but was in reality only a few seconds, for me to remember the little button in my pocket that Agent Andersen had given me to press if I felt things had gotten too dangerous.

I reached into my pocket and was about to press the button when suddenly there was an explosion of activity. Agents came from everywhere, sliding down ropes from the ceiling, coming in through the office door, coming from a secret door in a wall panel that had apparently been installed recently, up from a trap door in the floor, and through a door in the outside wall that had, until now, looked like a window. There must have been twenty to twenty-five agents, all with guns drawn, swarming my office in a matter of seconds, and surrounding Dimitri and his people. They immediately disarmed them and put handcuffs on their hands behind their backs.

One of the agents said, “Dimitri Petrovich, Galina Ikanov, Igor Dobrynin, and Sergey Yelochukof, you are all under arrest for the murders of Dominic Sobryan, Ana Sebetesky, Robert Jordan, and others to be named, in addition to fraud, intimidation, money laundering, illegal entry into the United States, carrying concealed weapons without permits, and additional unnamed crimes to be elicited at your arraignment and after a grand jury investigation. You have the right to remain silent. You have the right to …”

The agent finished reading them their rights, and they were all loaded into the waiting SWAT team vans and armored vehicles that had suddenly appeared in the parking lot adjacent to our building.

George, Katey, and I stood there stunned, our arms raised in the air, hardly believing what had just occurred right before our eyes.

Agent Andersen passed me and said with an almost monotone voice that he was sorry for the disruption this had caused and that he would get back to me to detail who these people really were, and exactly what some of the accusations had stemmed from.

I was amazed at how quickly it was all over. It was almost as if there had been a flash of light and everyone had swarmed into my office and then exited in what seemed like a few seconds. I assume it had taken at least several minutes, but it was as if time had stood still. Suddenly it was all over, almost everyone was gone, there was silence, and I was still shaking over what had happened and what could have happened.

George, Katey, and I tried to compose ourselves and determine what had happened. None of us could speak for several minutes.

I finally gathered my strength and asked, "Is everyone OK?"

We all started laughing simultaneously, which was probably just an emotional release from the tremendous tension and shock. George and Katey shook their heads, both to indicate they were OK and as a sign of disbelief.

"I think we should each relax in our offices for a while, and then take the last few hours of the day off, go home, and get some rest. See you all tomorrow morning here in the office, OK?"

They nodded in agreement, almost robotically. It was then that I realized I was drenched in sweat and shaking from cold at the same time. I got myself a drink of water and collapsed in my chair as George and Katey exited my office. I really could not do much. I reviewed some of my messages, listened to my voicemail, and looked at my emails and texts, as if in a haze, not totally comprehending any of these motions and tasks.

I wanted to be glad that this was all over, but I had a gut feeling that Dimitri and his people were just some small cogs in a larger gear, something deeper involving the Russian mafia and/or other connections. I did not have enough information to figure out exactly what had been going on and what might be coming, and for now, I didn't really care. These people had been handcuffed, arrested, and removed from our building, and that was all I could ask for right now.

The rest would have to wait until after the arraignment, so we got ourselves back together mentally and physically, and we moved forward with our plan to rebuild and expand the company.

It took several days for me to fully recover from the events that unfolded that day. We all got back to work and time seemed to speed up. I soon found myself in the back of a courtroom listening to the official sentencing for Cal, Herb, and Marty.

"Cal Donaven, Herb Henderson, and Marty Gilbert, please stand." They all stood up slowly.

"Cal Donaven, do you understand the charges brought against you?" the judge asked.

Cal nodded and gave a faint "yes."

"You have been convicted of complicity in attempted murder, theft, transporting stolen goods across state and national borders, hiding funds outside of the United States, failure to pay U.S. income tax, and other violations of U.S. law elicited in the complaint. I hereby sentence you to ten years in minimum-security prison, five years of probation, a fine equal to all illegally obtained gains in the amount of not less than $1 million. Be seated."

"Herb Henderson, do you understand the charges brought against you?" the judge asked.

"Yes, I do, your honor," Herb responded quietly.

"I hereby sentence you to one year in a minimum-security prison, five years of probation, a fine equal to all illegally obtained gains in the amount of not less than $1 million, and the loss of all ownership in SMI Automotive Inc., and all assets, including machinery and equipment, buildings, cash, accounts receivable, inventory, and stock. You are also forbidden to be associated with any automotive-related company or operation for an additional five years after your probation and prison sentence. Please sit down."

The judge continued. “Marty Gilbert, do you understand the charges brought against you?”

“Yes, I do, your honor,” he responded.

“I hereby sentence you to one year in a minimum-security prison, five years of probation, a fine equal to all illegally obtained gains in the amount of not less than one million dollars, and the loss of all ownership in SMI Automotive Inc., and all assets, including machinery and equipment, buildings, cash, accounts receivable, inventory, and stock. You are also forbidden to be associated with any automotive-related company or operation for an additional five years after your probation and prison sentence. Please sit down.”

A short time later, the three were led out of the court room and the judge said, “This court session is officially adjourned.”

I exited the courtroom and went back to the office. I then called Mitch, our attorney, to have him clarify exactly what the court hearing actually meant on a practical basis, and exactly what the status of the ownership of the company was and would be in the future. There was no point in working so hard if this was all going to be taken back by Herb, Marty, and Cal. Mitch explained to me that the ownership would immediately transfer into a court-supervised trust for a fixed period of time until the judge ruled on the ownership of the company.

Mitch also said that through informal conversations with the judge, he had determined that if we were successful, the ownership likely would be transferred from the trust to me and any of my designees. Cal, Herb, and Marty would be permanently out of the picture, no matter what happened.

Chapter 11

One problem down, more to come

Things slowly got back to normal. Sales were steadily picking up, and we were making slow but steady progress on our new products. One morning, I got a call from our chief engineer, Oscar Melton.

"Hey, chief," he began, "I think I finally solved the problem with our new bracket. Can I come up to talk to you about it now?"

"Of course, come on in," I responded.

Oscar was the typical "mad scientist"—hair going in every direction, unshaven, always dressed in a wrinkled shirt, plain khaki pants, mismatched socks, and black and white sneakers. He was, however, a brilliant scientist and a walking encyclopedia of metallurgy and engineering knowledge.

When he came in holding a few metal brackets with holes and slots through them and a file folder with papers hanging out, he said. "Well, Mr. Kirby, I think I finally came up with a new bracket with an entirely new steel chemistry that is twice the strength of the part it is replacing, and less than half the weight. The part can be extruded, and by using the extrusion dies to produce the slots and holes for the reduced material, there are almost no secondary operations to be done. It can also be stamped using traditional stamping dies."

"Have you sent it out for testing at one of our outside testing labs?" I asked.

"Yes, and they certified its strength, weight characteristics, steel chemistry, and extrusion capabilities. I have some samples here and all the data. I also have run some of this part on a prototype production line to make sure it was production-capable, and it passed with flying colors," he said.

"Oscar, is there any reason this cannot be used in military or aircraft applications?" I asked him.

"I don't see why not."

"Oscar, can you please get me a few samples and copies of your data? I want to run this all by our patent attorneys. I don't want to spend much more money until we are fully protected by a patent, or at least a patent pending."

"Will do, chief."

Oscar brought the samples and data to my office that afternoon. In the meantime, I had contacted our new patent attorneys and arranged for them to stop by to discuss the project with Oscar and me. I wanted to get on it right away, as I realized the tremendous potential it had in the marketplace and for our company.

Two days later, as I sat in my office with Oscar and our patent attorneys, Oscar described the new product.

"…and using this method, we can produce brackets, for example, with less than half the weight, and with twice the strength of conventional automotive bracket technology. In addition, and one of the best parts about all this, these brackets will cost less to produce than the ones they are replacing. I have provided each of you with a packet of information with the data I have collected from testing, a breakdown of the steel chemistry, and details of the process," Oscar said.

"Well, what do you think, fellas?" I asked the attorneys.

"This all looks pretty good. Of course, we will have to review all the details, but at first review, I see no problem patenting the process and the chemistry. We will, of course, do a search to make sure this has not already been patented, and if not, I think we are good to go," the attorney said.

"Great," I said, "and thanks, Oscar. Let's get on this right away and get it completed as soon as possible so that we can go forward on production." Then I told the attorneys, "In fact, I want you to make it a top priority to get the paperwork going to get initial patent pending status."

The next morning, with Oscar already sitting in my office, I called Katey in.

"Katey, can you come into my office and bring George with you?" I asked her on the phone. A few minutes later, she and George came in and sat down.

"I want to tell you both something that I believe will be a tremendous shot in the arm for the company, a real game changer. Oscar has come up with a new process for making undercarriage automotive brackets that I believe can turn into a tremendous revenue generator for us. In fact, I believe it could easily double or triple our revenue and our profits in just a few years. Oscar here will explain it to you."

Oscar then launched into his explanation of the new process, materials, and advantages. George and Katey were duly impressed.

"How soon will it be ready? How soon can we begin production? When can we begin selling these products?" George and Katey asked.

"I know you are both excited, but let's slow down a bit. We can't do anything until the patent process is finished, or at least until we get to 'patent pending' status. George, I want you to work closely with Oscar to determine our costs per unit in producing this new product. Katey, I want you to start feeling around with some of our customers as to how much demand there would be for this product, although I believe the demand would be almost unlimited. Down the road a bit, Katey, I will want you to begin looking into aircraft and military applications for this as well. George can help you with meeting the right people for this. I will begin speaking to our bankers to start looking for an increase in our line of credit and possibly long-term financing, as I believe this, if initially successful, will require major capital expenditures for new equipment, possibly robotic; additional inventory; and hiring. This has almost unlimited potential," I said.

I also told them clearly that this information was extremely confidential, with only those in the room, our attorneys, and CPA firm to know anything about it. We finished up and for the next few weeks, we ate, drank, and lived this new product every single day, pushing as hard as we could to get it ready for complete evaluation.

Sometime during that period, I received a call from Agent Andersen, explaining that Dimitri and his group had been removed to a distant and secret federal maximum-security facility, having been indicted, tried, and convicted. They had all been sentenced to lengthy prison terms and stiff penalties, and they would not be seen or heard from for a long, long time. He felt there was nothing for us to worry about, but just to be safe, the FBI was continuing the investigation into each individual in the group to find any connections to others inside or outside the U.S. He said he would continue to keep me informed.

Although I was grateful for his reassurances, not too long afterward, I began getting strange phone calls both directly and indirectly regarding our company. They all revolved around the potential sale of the company to a larger, as yet unnamed, entity.

It all started innocently one afternoon.

"Mr. Kirby? This is Mr. Glenn of Olson, Miller and Swath. We represent a buyer who is very interested in acquiring SMI Automotive. They are very, very interested and will make you an extremely attractive offer. When would you like to meet with them?"

"No, thank you. At the present time, it is completely out of the question, but thank you for the call," I quickly responded.

"Please take my name and phone number just in case you change your mind," Mr. Glenn said.

I thought nothing of it until I received a second, third, fourth, and fifth call from Mr. Glenn and from other companies. The calls and letters continued with greater frequency, and our law firm got similar inquiries. What had begun as a simple inquiry turned into an annoyance and, subsequently, into a serious concern.

Shortly afterward I received a call from our senior lending officer at the bank.

"Jason, how are you doing?" he asked.

"I am fine, very busy with the new product process. What's up?"

"Well, Jason, I want you to look at another company. They are in trouble financially. The owner has let the company slide, they are seriously behind on their mortgage and loan payments to us, and we very likely will have to pull the plug on them altogether, so we would like you to take a look at the company. We would really like SMI to purchase the company."

What?" I exclaimed. "Fred, you know how busy we are, getting the company back on track; getting our new products ready for market; cleaning up from the Russian fiasco; and the mess with Herb, Cal, and Marty. This is the last thing we need to get involved with!" I said.

"Listen Jason, I understand completely what you are saying, but would you just meet me over at the company, take a look around and listen to what we have to say? I would really appreciate it. They are in Aurora, Illinois, just a little over an hour from your office. How about I meet you out there about ten tomorrow morning?"

Reluctantly, I agreed.

At a few minutes to ten the next morning, I pulled into the lot at AMT, American Manufacturing Technologies.

Fred was standing next to his car in the lot, waiting for me.

"Hi, Jason. Glad you could make it. I know you will not be disappointed by what you will be seeing and will find this a very worthwhile trip," he said.

While I could not voice my true feelings, I felt I had a million better things to do this morning. But Fred had done so much for our company when we really needed it, and my curiosity had gotten the best of me.

We walked in and were greeted by Nancy Oustlinger, the general manager.

"Hi, Nancy," Fred began. "This is Jason Kirby, the gentleman I spoke to you about the other day. Can you please show us around and answer any questions he might have?"

"Of course," answered Nancy. Nancy was about five feet five inches in height but appeared to be very muscular. She had a deep voice and long, red hair. She was dressed in a practical blue blouse and blue jeans. She was extremely knowledgeable about her job and the company and glad to answer my questions. We began our tour in the office area, which was a mass of computer and other high-tech equipment where about fifteen clerical people were busy at their jobs. We then ventured into the plant area, where Nancy began her presentation. “We make highly sophisticated automation and robotic equipment for manufacturing, quality control, and shipping and receiving types of applications. Most of the equipment is proprietary in nature, which we have designed and custom-built specifically for our customers. While the company has been in business for over seventy years, our current management/ownership team has been in place for about eight years. Randy McQuade, our president and grandson of the founder, is not in right now. He is out of the country currently.”

We spent the next hour or so touring the approximately 135,000-square-foot facility. It was well- equipped and somewhat busy, but I sensed a certain feeling of hopelessness and low morale, although everyone seemed to be doing their jobs diligently.

We completed the tour, and Fred and I thanked her for her time and information.

Fred walked me to my car, where he asked, "Well, what do you think?"

"I'm not sure what you mean, Fred," I countered.

"I want to know what you think about what you just saw and if you would like to buy the company and straighten things out?" he said.

I took a deep breath and said, "Fred, you know we are knee-deep with a number of major initiatives, and the last thing I need on my plate is another headache to work on."

"Jason, I would not be pressing you on this, but the current owner/president, Randy McQuade, is not out of the country because of business. He is really busy sailing his boat in the Caribbean while the company is going under. He just doesn't care. More importantly, we have a major investment in this company in terms of substantial loans and we are about to cut them off. That would probably mean shutting down the entire operation, getting rid of all the employees, and selling all the assets to help satisfy at least a small portion of the liabilities and debt. We, the bank, would take a big loss, and all the employees would lose their jobs.

"What I am asking you to do, Jason, is just to take a look at the company, do your due diligence, and at least think about taking over the company. Believe me, the bank would make it extremely attractive for you to do so, in terms of exceptionally low interest rates and no initial investment on your part. You would be purchasing the company with, essentially, the assumption of only part of the debt and forgiveness of the balance of the debt. We would help you every step of the way.

"Their biggest problem is the current president and his lack of understanding or any concern about the company. He, of course, would be out of the picture permanently. He has plenty of money from his grandparents and parents, and basically no personal responsibility. He really doesn't care about anything else. We do believe the company is essentially sound and just needs someone like you and your management team and your expertise to turn things around. I know this is a very difficult time for you, but we have to make a decision in a relatively short period of time as to what we will do with the company and the debt. Would you please at least review things and think about it?" Fred said.

He was practically begging me to take a closer look at the company. I almost felt sorry for him and assumed, based on his discussion, that this company was a large part of his current loan portfolio and that the bank and Fred did not want to take a hit on the entire debt. Against my better judgment, I agreed to think about it. I did so for the entire drive back to the office.

On my drive back, I spoke with Bill, our CPA, about the potential AMT deal and asked him to arrange to review the records for some preliminary due diligence. I also contacted Mitch Conner so he would be prepared to review the company with regard to any potential legal issues, should we consider going forward.

I called Katey and George in to my office to let them know what was going on, and ask for their suggestions, questions, and concerns, but they really didn't have any at that moment other than the concern that we might be spreading ourselves too thin. I told them I agreed with them but that this might be an outstanding opportunity for us to expand our product base and diversify, and that the bank would bend over backward to help us make this happen. In addition, should we go ahead with the acquisition, it might help provide us with the automation equipment for our potential expansion and new product lines.

In the meantime, we found out we had received initial patent approval on our new material and bracket products so we could move forward immediately. I told Oscar to go ahead and investigate applications, testing, and other programs and told Katey to go ahead and sell some of the new brackets so we could begin getting orders in the pipeline. As soon as that happened, we could begin ordering the machines and tooling to produce these products. I met with George to make sure we would be able to finance the new equipment, inventory, and tooling as well as have enough support for accounts payable and receivable for the initial term of about twelve months until sales and revenue ramped up to pay down the loans and provide working capital for the new products. I felt that the sky was the limit with these items' potential.

The new bracket program was going well, and we began our review of the AMT project, but the contacts from "potential buyers" increased and, at the same time, became more elusive. Although we were getting these directly via other attorneys, through our attorneys, and even through George, all were unsolicited and with no particular potential buyer identified.

I spoke with our CPAs, attorneys, and George and Katey. Their opinions of the situation were a mixed bag. Our attorneys and CPAs felt it might be worthwhile to investigate these inquiries without providing a definite response, Katey was concerned about the way it was happening, and George wanted to at least pursue some of the offers to see if anything concrete came of it. I was uncertain and felt we should begin checking into the validity of these "offers."

I decided to take a multifaceted approach to find out if there was anything worthwhile in these offers, to determine who or what was behind them, why they were all making these offers now, and, most importantly, where these people were getting their information about our company. To reduce the risk of losing our focus on increasing our sales and revenue, our intense new product development program, and the AMT deal, I asked Bill and Mitch to follow up on these offers, investigate the sources of the inquiries, and keep me apprised of what they found.

While requests to purchase the company continued to come in, our attorneys and CPAs were running into dead ends. Although they agreed to have conversations with potential buyers, they could not find out exactly who the buyers were. In virtually every case, they were told that the buyers would be revealed when we submitted our financial statements for their review. Of course, we refused to do so. We were at a stalemate. I considered bringing in outside investigators or governmental agencies, but I decided against it as it would further divert our focus at such a critical time.

Katey was receiving excellent preliminary responses to potential sales of our new brackets. Oscar's preliminary testing was going well. I gave George the go-ahead to place some orders for prototype quantities of the special steel from our usual sources.

A few days later, I asked him how the orders were coming and he said, "I can't seem to find this steel available anywhere. I contacted six different steel warehouses and mills, and they all said they cannot produce it for us. I don't understand it, but it is very strange."

"Well, expand your potential suppliers. Look out of state and out of the country if you have to," I said. "We need to jump on this quickly to get these new products into the market as soon as possible and, at the very least, get samples to customers so they can begin evaluating applications and, hopefully, placing orders."

"I will try again," he responded.

In the meantime, Katey was continuing to get very positive responses from our current and potential customers, both in the OEM arena and with aftermarket parts manufacturers.

Several more days went by, and I had not heard from George. "How is it going with those steel orders we spoke about, George?" I asked.

"I still can't find anyone that will produce this steel for us. I don't know what to do."

"Have you checked out of state, out of the region?" I asked.

"I have looked all across the country and Canada and had no luck," he answered.

"Well, keep looking. We really need this material."

I decided to make a few inquiries of my own. I called an old friend, Frank Parsons, president of American Steel Company Inc., an electric mini-mill in Chattanooga, Tennessee.

"Frank, how are you doing? I know I haven't spoken to you for quite some time," I said.

"Jason, how have you been? I really miss working with you, even after all these years. How have you been? What can I do for you?"

"Well, Frank, I need a little favor. What is the smallest and largest tonnage you can run at a time?" I asked him.

"Well, right now we can do from about one ton up to about five ton, but in a few weeks, we will be starting up our new furnace expansion, and we will be able to go up to about a twenty-five-ton maximum. What do you need?"

"Initially, I need about five tons of a special chemistry. I am emailing that to you right now. Would you be able to run this?"

"Hmm, let me look this over. … Yes, we can do that, but we are pretty busy right now. When do you need this?"

"Frank, I really need this yesterday. Can you do this run for me? If this all works out, I will need a lot more later on."

"For you, yeah, I'll do it. I should be able to have it in your hands within a week. Will that work?"

"Yes, I can live with that; however, I need to ask you a few additional favors to go along with this. First, I can't send you an official purchase order. I will send you an email with my signature on it. Will that be OK?"

"Sure, if I can't trust you, I don't know anyone I can trust. What is this all about?"

"I really can't tell you right now, so please just keep this all under your hat, and I promise I will explain it all to you down the road. I will, of course, make sure you get paid, but I need you to only contact me if you have any questions, need shipping information, and so on. Do you mind?"

"Yes, I can live with that."

"Frank, I do need to ask you one last thing. I will make sure you get paid, but again I will need you to keep this all totally confidential, just between you and me for a while. Is that OK?"

"Jason, if it's you asking, it is all right with me. I will get right on it, and I will deal with the paperwork however is best for you."

"Thanks, Frank. I really appreciate this. If you need me for any reason, please contact me on my private cell phone. You have the number. Thanks again. I really do appreciate this."

"Jason, this doesn't even begin to repay you for all you have done for me over the years."

"Thanks, Frank."

George continued to try to place orders for the steel we needed, and, in the meantime, the steel came in from American Steel. I made sure Oscar got the steel, and, as best as I could, made sure no one else knew about the shipment. I needed to keep this all quiet until I got to the bottom of what was going on.

At the same time, Fred was still pressing me about purchasing AMT. I had received a few additional voicemails from Fred about the potential deal. I finally called him back and told him that, although the AMT deal looked interesting, I really could not deal with it right now. If he could give me a few months to launch our new products, I would have a little more time to look at it. He reluctantly agreed.

I could not, of course, let him know about the difficulty of purchasing steel for the brackets, my thoughts and suspicions about who was behind it, or the true scope of what these new brackets could mean. For the time being, I had to make sure we focused on operating and growing the company and getting our new products into production and into the marketplace.

Oscar had begun testing and prototyping brackets with the new steel from American Steel, and that had gone successfully. There were, of course, some initial problems, a period of debugging, and so on.

Once he got good samples, I provided them to Katey, who pushed customers to get some hard orders, and she was extremely successful. Both OEM and aftermarket customers were enthused about the brackets. They were thrilled by an opportunity to cut vehicle weight, thereby increasing gas mileage, as well as cut costs.

As soon as we saw the reception Katey was getting, we began looking for new equipment, redesigned the plant floor to accommodate it, and arranged for inventory space. At the same time, I placed our next, larger order with Frank at American Steel and had another conversation with him.

"Hi, Frank. How are you doing?"

"I am doing well, Jason. Good to hear from you. I trust our steel met your expectations?"

"Absolutely. I need to place another order for twenty-five tons, and I also need to pick your brain. The success we had with your steel presents us with another kind of problem. On the one hand, we like your steel and need more. On the other hand, your production limitations mean we will not be able to get the actual quantities we will need in the future when production ramps up. Can you recommend one or two mills or warehouses that would be able to provide me with at least fifty tons of the steel a month?"

"Whoa, that's a tall order. Let me check around with some people I know to see if I can source that order for you."

"Frank, please keep in mind, I still need to keep this all under the radar. Any inquires you make, please don't mention me or the company's name or the products it will get used for. Until I get to the bottom of the issues I have here, I need to keep this completely quiet. Do you mind?"

"No problem, Jason. I completely understand. I'll get back to you in a few days."

I started digging deeper into the steel issue. I called some of the local steel warehouses and regional mills myself. As George had told me, some said they could not produce the steel for us; on the other hand, a number of them said they would be glad to accommodate us. Now I was even more confused. I asked a few friends in the business to follow up with the mills that refused to try to get a sense of why they could not. I anxiously awaited their replies, but I also knew it would take a few days because they would be getting information from "inside" these organizations.

I still had a nagging feeling that Herb and Marty were somehow behind this through their attorneys, but I had no way to prove my theory, or even justify it. Maybe the results of my indirect inquiries would give me an indication of what was really going on.

"Jason, Max Gardner here." Max was an old friend who had been in the metal stamping business for over thirty years. I knew I could trust him and had asked for his assistance.

"I made some inquiries like you asked me to with people inside a few of the steel suppliers that rejected your order requests and found that they have plenty of steel. The people I spoke with were told simply not to process the order. No reason was given, or background explanation, or anything. I am going to move higher up within these organizations to see if I can find out anything else. I'll get back to you as soon as I hear anything more."

"Thanks, Max. I really appreciate this."

"No problem. You owe me one," Max said.

Some of the others I had contacted checked in, and the answers were the same. The rejections were correct, but no explanation was given.

I was back at square one. We were getting our initial shipments of steel from Frank at American Steel, and Frank had provided me with a few names of larger mills that might provide us with the quantities we would need to produce enough brackets to fill our orders. As I went down the list, contacting each mill, I realized I would have to set up circuitous routes to get the steel to us until we could resolve the issue. In one instance, I found a mill in India, and we simply shipped the steel to a warehouse in London. From there, it would travel to New York, and then to a steel warehouse in Louisville, then on to our facility. I created a new company to which the steel would ultimately be shipped, and that name would appear on all documents so as not to arouse suspicion.

With the two orders from American Steel, Oscar was able to produce enough testing, prototype, and preproduction brackets for Katey to get plenty of advance orders. We then began ordering equipment and planning for its installation. I placed the large orders with the steel mill in India and with another one Frank had found for me in Canada. While we did that, we continued to look for some domestic suppliers. Until we found them, I used the same type of routing system to bring the steel in.

"Hey, boss, what's with these new parts? I am still waiting for the quality specs from Oscar so I can begin testing them. Will we be seeing larger quantities? Do I need to set up some new procedures? How soon will I need to do so?" Billy asked.

"Yes, we will need to set up some procedures for these new parts. I will get with Oscar, and he will let you know what to do," I answered.

Why was Billy asking so many questions all of a sudden? I wondered if he was involved. My mind was racing with different thoughts and scenarios, most with no good foundation. I didn't know if my thoughts were legitimate or I was becoming exceptionally paranoid. I contacted Oscar, told him to come to my office, briefed him on our needs, and told him to keep close watch on Billy.

At the same time, I alerted Anna, our materials manager that a great deal more of the type of steel we were using for the brackets would be coming in. I told her to let me know when more arrived. I wanted it kept isolated in a fenced, secure area. Anna was a short, quiet, dark-haired woman of average build, about forty-five years old, with an excellent knowledge of shipping and materials. I had learned to depend on her and make full use of her knowledge and experience.

At that point, I decided to regularly review security tapes from inside the plant to see if anything unusual was happening, particularly with regard to the new steel and the preproduction parts. I became suspicious of everyone. I did not know who my enemy was and who my friend was. There was, in fact, no way to know. Until I was able to determine who was behind it all—the continuous attempts to purchase the company, the roadblocks to purchasing steel for our new products, and who knew what else—I had to remain vigilant to protect myself and the company without becoming overly suspicious. But I could not hide in a dark room. I had to be out and about, involved in the company, and always watching.

Katey was bringing in orders for our new products, and the new equipment was arriving and being installed. At the same time, the large orders of steel from India and Canada were arriving, bringing additional inquiries from employees. Some were innocent curiosity, but some were likely industrial espionage. The key was to determine which was which.

I reviewed the internal security tapes daily, but nothing was occurring that was obvious or unusual. After a few months, we finally received our first hard orders for the new brackets, and began production to fill them. New orders came in as fast we were able to produce product. While this was gratifying, it strained our existing resources and created the need to hire employees. Although the new bracket production line was highly automated with automatic presses and feeds, robotic welding and transfer operations, and other robotic functions, it still required supervision and maintenance.

I decided to bring in a third-party organization I was familiar with to act as program manager for the completion of installation and setup of the new lines, including hiring and training the new employees and overseeing production for a while. Our current resources were stretched to the limit, and I believed implementing a new program at this time would push us over the edge. I had worked with Allied Program Management and its president, Stan Fulton, and I fully trusted him. Stan had a Ph.D. from an Ivy League university, many years of experience in automotive and manufacturing, and a five-star reference list, having worked for most of the major automotive companies, the U.S. military, the U.S. government, foreign governments, and some of the best think tanks. Allied's work was impeccable, thorough, and complete, and I knew Stan would keep me up to date every step of the way and his results would be A-plus.

Chapter 12

A Major Loss

As this change was being implemented, taking a little of the pressure off of me, I had time to reflect on our steel procurement issues as well as contemplate the potential AMT purchase. This particular morning, I was deep in thought, having completed my morning meetings, when April called to let me know Phil Forman was in the lobby waiting to see me.

I was stunned. I had known Phil since we were kids in elementary school together, and we had kept in touch all these years—first by phone and letter, and later by email and text. I had, however, not seen Phil for many years. When it had come time for each of us to go off to college, I went to a local university to study business, and Phil went to Harvard and MIT to study advanced sciences. He had doctorates in biochemical engineering and genetics and had done post-doc work in genetic engineering. He was director of biogenetic research and engineering at Talbot University in Nebraska, and he also headed his own biogenetic research and commercialization company.

Because of Phil's research, many thousands of people's lives had been saved with genetically designed medications and treatments, and many millions more were alive due to his research and development of genetically modified foods that can grow with extremely limited water resources and within extreme temperature ranges. He had a wife and two adult daughters and a few grandchildren. I could not imagine why he was in the lobby unless he just happened to be in town on business, but I told April to send him right in.

As Phil, a tall man of about 180 pounds with a balding head, entered my office, I greeted him warmly and told him to sit down.

"Phil, how are you? What are you doing in town? How are Melissa and the girls and, of course, the grandchildren?" I asked.

"They are all fine. It is good to see you again after so many years. You look great, and it looks like you are very busy, so I will get right to the point." Phil was always black and white, and direct and to the point. There were no shades of grey for Phil, maybe because he was so brilliant and saw everything from a factual, logical perspective.

"Jason, I came here today to ask a favor."

"Of course, Phil, anything I can do to for you I will be glad to. You know that," I responded.

"Yes, of course I do, and that is why I came. I need you to promise me you will help Melissa and the girls with any of their business or financial needs."

"Phil, I don't know where this is coming from, but I am sure you and the girls have financial advisers, CPAs, attorneys, and those kinds of people already. Why would you need me to do this all of a sudden?"

"Jason, of course I knew I could depend on you; I just needed to hear it from you directly. You see, I am dying. I have up to a year to live, and I wanted to get all my affairs in order, and you are the most trusted friend I have. I need to know you will be there for them when and if they need you."

I felt like someone had just kicked me in the stomach. I was speechless, and I ached with shock.

Phil looked at me with astonishment. For him, it was all facts and objectivity.

I just didn't know what to say.

"Jason, do you understand what I just told you? Will you be able to do it?" Phil asked. I finally managed to get a few words out.

"Of course, Phil, I will do this. But forgive me. I am totally stunned. I certainly did not expect this. What is going on?"

"Well, about a year or so ago, I was doing some research with radioactive plutonium isotopes on plant genes. Somehow, something leaked, and I was exposed to some of the radiation. It entered my blood immediately. The doctors were able to slow the advancing damage of the radiation to my body, but that was all they could do. Now it is just a matter of time until it impacts all my cells. I go for regular treatments to filter and clean my blood, and that slows down the pending damage but does not stop it. There have been many advances in radiation poisoning treatment but, unfortunately, not enough to save me."

I sat in stunned silence. Phil was brilliant, and I was sure he had explored every possible avenue, researched everything available, and tried to figure out a path of treatment on his own. Still, there had to be something.

"Jason, could I take a tour of the plant?" he asked. He must have noticed I was off in thought and decided to bring me back to earth. "You know, I have never been through an operating manufacturing facility, particularly an automotive-related one."

It took me a few seconds to come back to reality.

"Of course, Phil. Come with me."

As he stood, I directed him to the door into the plant area, and I provided him with safety glasses and ear protection plugs. I pointed out some of the operations and areas, including shipping and receiving, the stamping presses, welding and grinding operations, painting and drying operations, and so on. We walked slowly, and he took in everything with interest and enjoyment. He had many pointed questions, which was not unexpected, knowing the kind of person he was.

When we finished and came back into the office, he hugged me and said his driver was waiting to take him to the airport. He had to fly to Cleveland to see someone and then back home. When he hugged me, I felt how skinny he had become. The 180-pound man I had known for many years was probably closer to 130 pounds now, and that added to my concern. His jacket had hidden his substantial weight loss. He made me reiterate my promise to look after Melissa and the girls, and I did so. I told him I would be in touch soon, and he seemed surprised but happy at that promise, and accepted it at face value.

As Phil walked out the door, I wondered if I would have the privilege of seeing him again. Would he be able to improve and get well, or was his assessment of the situation correct, and there was nothing to be done? While these questions swirled in my head, I felt an emptiness as I watched a good friend walk out the door, probably for good. It hurt. I went back to my desk and sat motionless for what seemed like hours but what was, in reality, only a few minutes.

Then I picked up the phone and called Melissa. "Melissa, this is Jason. How are you doing? How are the girls doing?" I asked in a rapid succession of questions, still shaken by my visit with Phil.

"We are all fine and dealing with the situation. How are you?" she asked, more concerned about me than herself.

"I just want you to know that Phil was here, and he asked that I be available for you and the girls and their families should anything come up of a business or financial nature that you could use an extra opinion on, have something to take care of, or anything like that. I am always here for you, Melissa," I said, not even knowing that words were coming out of my mouth.

"Thanks, Jason. I know you care about Phil and us, and I know very well that you will be available. I also know as time goes on we will have many questions and concerns, and I won't hesitate to call you, but thank you for the reassurance. We need all the support we can get right now as we try to get through all of this," she went on.

"Don't forget. Call me whenever you need to, Melissa."

"Thanks, Jason. I will. You have always been there for Phil and us. All the best," she concluded.

As the weeks and months passed, I stayed in touch with Melissa on a regular basis, and she was always appreciative. Whenever I thought about her and Phil, I had a sinking feeling in my stomach that would be the day I would receive bad news. The thought just sits at the back of your mind, and you're always hoping it will not occur, but you know very well that it is a reality. Then you push it back to the far corner of your mind until the next time.

One day several months later, I was reading over some financial reports when the dreaded call came. "Jason, this is Melissa. It's over. Can you come?"

While I had known this dreaded day would come, I never was really mentally prepared. After what seemed like an eternity, I finally gathered the strength to respond to Melissa.

"What is going on, Melissa?" I asked, almost oblivious to the words coming out of my mouth.

"It's all over. We lost Phil late last night. He went peacefully in his sleep. Can you come? I am totally lost, I don't know what to do, what to say ..." Her words trailed off into silence.

"Of course, I will get a flight today. I will be there by tonight," I said. "See you soon, Melissa."

I already felt empty at the loss of this good friend. I called Amy and told her to get me a flight as soon as possible.

****

As I stood in the pouring rain at the cemetery the next day, the casket of my good friend, Phil, was slowly lowered into the ground to his final resting place. As I thought about what now would be our permanent separation, with the loss of friendship and conversation, his intellectual pursuits, his creativity, an enormous void was created in my heart and body, and I began to sob and shake, ever more violently and uncontrollably.

Melissa came over and hugged me, as did her two daughters. We all stood there for what seemed an eternity, and eventually, I sensed other people speaking, and Melissa and the girls slowly released their embrace. As the crowd began to disperse, I found myself virtually alone.

Melissa and the girls were still nearby, quietly speaking to the last of the friends and relatives who had come to be with them, and I reiterated my offer.

"Melissa, remember if you or the girls need me for anything, I am only a phone call away, whatever and whenever it is."

They acknowledged my offer and wandered over to their cars and drivers. I slowly walked to my rental car for the very lonely drive back to the airport and the even lonelier flight home. I guess it was better that way, as I was in no mood to speak to anyone, with the tremendous hole that had opened in my heart and body. By evening I was back in my home, almost oblivious to the outside world. I knew I would have to immerse myself in my work for quite some time to emotionally survive this event.

I got into the office very early the next morning, having had little sleep the night before. As I delved into my work, I remembered that as our production volumes, sales revenue and profitability were increasing with our new products, we were having increasing difficulty obtaining steel. Frank at American Steel was barely keeping up with our needs, and he was already at capacity, unable to increase production for us. The additional suppliers I had set up through circuitous routes were not dependable enough, and their material took too long to reach us. We needed another supplier and, at the same time, I needed to find out why we could not obtain our steel anywhere else.

J.T. Palace

I was about to contact the private investigator we had used in the past, but then I realized I needed to find someone I could really trust to investigate this problem. I had to find a person who had no connections to anyone inside or outside the company, so that I could get an unbiased investigation. I contacted some old friends with whom I had done business a number of years ago and whom I could completely trust, and explained my predicament.

I was also concerned that someone might even be listening in on my conversations, so I left the premises and, from a parking lot a few miles away, I called our old FBI contacts. I asked them to come in and sweep our entire facility for any electronic devices that could be recording conversations, emails, or texting. I realized I sounded paranoid, but I had to get to the bottom of this problem because it was directly affecting the viability of the company. Then, one of my old trusted business associates provided me with the name of an individual he felt was trustworthy and independent, Ron Eppler. He was a former Army intelligence officer who had gone to the CIA, who was now semiretired and doing independent private investigations. He seemed the perfect fit, and I arranged to meet him a day later at a small restaurant about a half-hour drive from our office.

The next day, as I was drinking a cup of tea in the restaurant, a slight, medium-size man in his fifties with metal-rimmed glasses who was wearing a very nice suit, white shirt, and tie approached me. He introduced himself as Ron Eppler. He was certainly not what I had expected, having imagined a six-foot-four-inch Marine type of individual, but after speaking with him, I was convinced he was a perfect choice.

"I'm Ron Eppler. Are you Jason?" he asked.

"Yes, please sit down, Ron. Let me explain the situation. When I have finished, I would like to hear your thoughts," I said.

Then I briefly gave him the entire history of the situation, including the criminal activities of Marty, Herb, and Cal; our new management team; our new product line; the events with the Russians; and our issues with trying to purchase steel, our critical commodity.

"So Ron, I want to address, once and for all, who or what is behind all of this and end the problems completely so we can go forward and run this company as it should be."

I waited for his analysis and solutions. Ron was quiet for a moment and then he began. "I fully understand what you have told me, and it certainly sounds like your problems may be from the inside, the outside, or both. What I will need to do is to evaluate exactly what is going on and with whom. It may take listening devices, security recordings, and many other secret investigational processes to get to the bottom of this—and I will because I understand how critical this all is to you and your organization. To answer what you are probably thinking right now: Yes, I can do this. And yes, I will do this."

"I am very glad to hear that," I said, "but I would like to know what your approach will be, how you will do this, and what type of time frame you anticipate. I really don't want to stretch this whole thing out for too long. In other words, exactly what are your thoughts on this? How will you approach this?" I asked.

"Well," Ron began, "of course, I will need to evaluate exactly what is going on, but how about if I meet with you again one week from today so that I can provide you with my plan in detail? I will need to determine, as you mentioned, if there are any listening and/or recording devices at this operation or near your facility. I also will need to check phone records, cell phone and text conversations, and those kinds of things to give me a direction to go in. We really need to know if this issue is from the inside, outside, or both; how it is being perpetrated; and who is responsible. Then we can decide what we are going to do about it. I really believe this is doable to completion in a relatively short period of time, and I will lay that all out for you next week when we meet. Does that sound all right?" he said.

"It sounds fine to me. I look forward to meeting with you next week to hear your plan of attack," I said. We discussed a few more things about the company, including the people on our management team, and I promised to provide him with a complete employee list by the next day. We also discussed vendors who were not willing to supply us with steel and other pertinent facts. We finished and went our separate ways.

I was a little concerned about what methods this investigation might entail, particularly regarding his contacts and how he might obtain some of the information he mentioned. I also knew the old adage "fight fire with fire," might well apply to this situation. To identify the source of our problems might take more drastic measures, and I fully believed Ron was the person for the job.

The week passed quickly as I spent long hours at the office, following up on a number of project meetings, and other things I had previously left to subordinates. I also was in touch with Melissa to see how she was doing and to offer any assistance I could. Production continued to ramp up on our new product line, and demand was continuing to increase, as were requests for similar products using our new technology. All of that put more pressure on our steel needs and production capacity, leading me to believe we would soon need to expand our current facility to accommodate the growth. I decided not to do anything about that until we had the larger issues resolved, hopefully sooner rather than later with Ron's help.

Ron and I arranged to meet at another small restaurant about twenty minutes from the office. I arrived a few minutes early, only to find that he was already at a table waiting for me.

"Hi, Jason. Good to see you." We shook hands and he began. "I want to get right down to business because my initial research tells me I have many avenues to explore," he said. "First, I want to check for any listening or recording devices that are currently operating inside or near your facility. I plan to bring in a small crew of experts whom I have worked with many times for this type of operation. We will come in as energy-savings experts, trying to determine how the company can save money on various energy uses, including air leaks, insulation, electronic HVAC controls, even machine controls and associated electrical and gas usage, general electrical loss, and similar types of things. This will give us access to every inch of your facility without drawing any particular attention.

"You will let your management team know in advance about our anticipated visit, so they will be expecting us. Our vehicles will have an established energy reduction company name on them, just in case someone checks up on us. The company name will have an established history, so there is nothing to worry about. At the same time, we will be installing certain small devices to begin picking up interchanges from inside and outside the company, and will also be installing very small and virtually unobservable cameras throughout the facility so we can monitor any questionable activity from outside your building. I know this all sounds very intrusive, but this is really the only way we can do this properly and completely.

"Finally, I have small teams already primed to begin investigating any questionable employees, some of your vendors, and certainly what should have been potential steel vendors to work on that front to determine why you have had so much difficulty trying to obtain steel. Again, I know this all sounds like a secret paramilitary, covert intelligence operation, which, in reality, it is. We plan on leaving no stone unturned until we find out what and who is at the bottom of all this. Does this all sound all right to go forward on?"

It took me a little while to digest all that he had said, but I knew that although this was a very deliberate and detailed plan, and that I had some discomfort with the paramilitary intelligence feel of the whole operation, we really had no choice but to complete the plan properly as soon as possible.

"Ron, go ahead right away. Let's get this thing taken care of right now." Ron said goodbye and we both left.

At my regular weekly management meeting, I advised the team that an energy analysis company would be coming in shortly. I told them the analysts would be examining the entire building, including plant, office, storage areas, machinery and equipment, and HVAC systems, as well as the exterior. I said it matter-of-factly, telling them that it was important for us to work on becoming more energy-efficient. I indicated that, as energy costs were expected to continue to escalate and we would be using more energy as we increased production, energy efficiency was a good place to begin. One of the attendees asked the name of the company, which I provided. Everyone seemed fine with the idea as it was presented.

I was in contact with Ron several times in the interim, planning the date and time his team would arrive, getting additional information to him, and planning for his work while he and his team were on-site. At the same time, although steel supplies continued to tighten due to our increased demand, Frank at American Steel did his best to supply us with what we needed. He had his facility running at and over capacity, using additional shifts just to keep us supplied until we could arrange for alternate vendors. I also spoke with architects, engineers, and contractors about putting a sizable addition onto our building to increase production capacity as our sales continued to expand and were expected to do so for the foreseeable future.

Within a week, Ron and his team came on-site to begin their complete energy analysis. I had to admit that they looked very legitimate, with their vehicles, shirts, and paperwork prominently displaying the name of their company. They worked all day and into the evening, covering every inch of our building and, at the same time, installing their monitoring and surveillance equipment. I could not determine exactly where any of it was without Ron pointing it out to me.

After that, I had to wait, albeit impatiently, for Ron to get back to me with the results of his investigation and analysis. He told me it would take a few weeks, and in the interim, he said he would also bring me a thorough energy analysis report to make sure there were no questions about what he and his team were really doing. About two weeks later, Ron presented his energy analysis to me and my team at one of our regular weekly meetings. His report was thorough and genuine, pointing out energy losses, recommendations, and quotes for additional energy conservation work. The second report came about a week later with a call from Ron. "Jason, this is Ron. How are you doing? Listen, I need to meet with you again to go over my findings and present you with some additional quotations and information. Can you meet me at the same place we first met at a few weeks ago?"

"Sure, Ron, can we meet at eight thirty tomorrow morning there?"

"Sure, see you tomorrow."

I knew his terminology was deliberate to disguise the real reason for our meeting. The morning could not come fast enough for me. I was eager to, hopefully, finally get the answers I needed to continue our business. As I drove to the restaurant, my mind was spinning in every direction with potential scenarios. What had Ron found? Who or what was responsible for all of this? Were foreign agents involved? Was it competitors? Disgruntled employees? Even secret government investigators? I just didn't know what to think, but I was extremely agitated about the possible answers. The thirty-minute drive seemed endless, but I finally arrived at the restaurant, where Ron was waiting for me.

"Hi, Jason. I have a lot of material to get through, so let's start immediately. Are you ready to hear what I have found?"

"I am very nervous about what you have found but really want to hear all about it," I said.

"Well, let's begin. As you know, we did a thorough inspection of your entire facility for listening devices, recording devices, and exposure to outside monitoring. We also interviewed and reviewed a number of employees and former employees, as well as some of the vendors that refused to provide you with steel. In addition, we spent a lot of time reviewing emails, texts, phone calls, and phone records to help us determine who might be involved in all of this. What we found is somewhat complex and agitating, but I will give you all the various parts and how they fit together.

"First, let me begin with the outer rings and then work my way in. Before I begin, however, I want to caution you that you should not act on any of the information I will be providing you without consulting your legal counsel, and the appropriate federal and local law enforcement agencies. You do not want to act alone and, as a result, potentially jeopardize all of our work and the very real possibility of proper accusations, convictions, criminal and civil lawsuits, indictments, and potential incarcerations of some of the individuals involved. Jason, do you understand why I have told you this?

"Yes, of course," I answered quickly.

"OK, then let's begin. Do you remember quite some time ago, you were approached and threatened by some Russian agents and so-called business owners, including Mr. Petrovich from the Russian Automotive Group? Well, although he and some of his associates were arrested, convicted, and imprisoned, some of his successors were still interested in your company. They were in touch with your old buddies, Herb, Marty, and Cal, even during their incarceration. That consortium was responsible for using various types of electronic surveillance and monitoring of your and the company's activities, all in an effort to disrupt activities of the company and ultimately take over the company at little or no cost. They would not have been able to do all this without the assistance of your old CPA and a few people from your old management team. We have identified all of them and accumulated enough evidence to indict and, I believe, convict all of them in court for criminal activities, as well as send them away for a very long time.

"In speaking with some associates, we also believe there is sufficient evidence to set the stage for substantial civil lawsuits with significant monetary damages. Now, associated with all of this, I found that some of these same individuals were involved in a scheme to prevent some vendors from selling steel to you through the use of bribes and harassment. We have spoken to representatives of these companies, and they are more than willing to testify against these people on behalf of your company and you, most of them to avoid prosecution themselves. As an aside, we have disabled what we believe to be all of the electronic surveillance equipment and removed it from your site and are keeping it as evidence should you decide to file formal charges against any or all of these people. Thus far, we have not notified any law enforcement agencies or U.S. intelligence services of what has transpired. Those things can be done a little later. Do you have any questions at this point?" Ron asked.

"I know this is a lot to comprehend and digest all at once, particularly finding out all who were involved," he continued.

I took a deep breath, thought about what he had told me, and said, "Yes, I heard everything you said, but am still having difficulty processing everything. There is a good deal of shock and certainly a great deal to digest."

"OK, then I will tell you about the final piece of the puzzle and, again, whatever I tell you, please listen carefully to what I say, but do not even plan on pursuing anything until we discuss this all further and you have the discussions I suggested with your legal counsel and the proper authorities. Agreed?"

I heard the word "yes" come out of my mouth, but I was still stunned by the information Ron had presented to me so far.

"OK, now I will continue. It really bothered my team and me that you were not able to purchase steel. It made no sense. It had nothing to do with the financial strength of the company, the quantity you needed, or anything else that was apparent to us, so we started digging deeper and deeper to find out the root source and, finally, we found it. We examined specific landline and cell phone records as well as text records. We found that steel companies did not refuse your orders; they were instructed to not accept your orders. Their instructions came from inside the company." There was a long pause before Ron continued. “Specifically from your CFO George Montry.”

I was stunned. My jaw dropped and I did not know what to say. Initially, I assumed it was all a misunderstanding that Ron was completely wrong, that he had mixed up George with someone else. But the more I thought about it and the more evidence Ron showed me, including recordings he played and texts he showed me, I realized this was no mistake. George was responsible.

As Ron had suggested, I decided I would do nothing at this point. We discussed several potential strategies to deal with George and the rest of those involved, trying to come up with a good solution to take care of everyone at the same time, not arouse any suspicion, prevent a recurrence, and put an end to this entire affair. I told Ron I would speak with our attorneys immediately, and he indicated he would speak with his direct contacts in the FBI, CIA, and Justice Department. We said our goodbyes and, armed with the documentation Ron had provided me, I drove directly to our attorney’s office, calling him from the parking lot of the restaurant before I left.

“Hi Mitch,” I began when I arrived at his office. “I need to discuss something with you that is extremely confidential and that, although we cannot move on this immediately, I want you to be able to move on it quickly when we are ready."

"Sure, Jason," Mitch responded. I recounted all that had transpired in the past few weeks, and all that Ron had done and told me about. Mitch was stunned but understood the importance of taking care of all this properly so that we could successfully prosecute all those involved. He explained the legal ramifications of what was to come, and what we could and could not do. I put him in touch with Ron, and I told him to work directly with Ron and his contacts as we formulated and executed a plan. Mitch was satisfied, and I returned to the office.

"Hi, George. How are you today?" I asked George Montry as I stepped into his office.

"Very busy but good. What's up?" he asked.

"You know we are extremely tight on our steel supplies as our production has increased dramatically. The small prototype quantities we have been able to get are nowhere near what we need now, let alone in the future. Have you had any success finding any vendors for us?" I asked.

"No, not a single one that I have contacted can supply us," he said.

"Did you try local, domestic, Canada? How many sources did you contact?"

"Yes, of course. I must have contacted close to twenty with no luck," he answered.

"Well, keep trying, maybe some in South and Central America. We really need that steel. Also, if we can get the steel, I want to begin working on a building expansion to accommodate our increased demand. Look at the other potential steel sources and also begin looking at finding some additional space or new buildings. It may pay to just move to a larger facility," I told him.

"OK, will do," he answered.

I thanked him and went to my office.

I now had fully convinced myself that Ron was correct. Over the next few weeks, Ron worked diligently to put his plan together and make sure everything went down perfectly. We met one more time at the same restaurant a few weeks later to confirm everything before executing our plan with all the agencies and people involved. We determined the date and time that everything would happen simultaneously. Warrants were prepared and signed, all agencies were notified, including Homeland Security, Justice Department, FBI, CIA, local authorities, as well as Ron's team. The only people associated with the company who were aware of what was happening were me and our attorneys. Now it was only a matter of time.

On the appointed day, warrants were executed on Herb, Marty, and Cal (who was still in prison), representatives of the Russian Automotive Group, and a few former employees of the company. The FBI, CIA, Homeland Security, and local law enforcement officials executed all of the warrants at the same time. In addition, agents and law enforcement authorities came into the office and presented a warrant to George. While there was satisfaction that all of this was coming to an end, it hurt to know that someone so close to me, whom I had trusted and treated like a partner, would do this to me and the company.

The results of the interrogations of all of the accused would take a while, but then I could learn the full extent of what had happened and why.

While I waited, I worked quickly. I called Bill, the CPA, and brought him up to date on all that had transpired and told him I needed one of his people to come in as an acting CFO.

"Besides that, Bill, I need you to recruit a new CFO for us. Aside from his or her capabilities, I need them to be honest, pragmatic, and ethical."

"I completely understand and would expect nothing less, Jason. I will have one of our staff CPAs come in as a temporary CFO and begin the recruiting process immediately. A few names come to mind right away, but I will check with them to see if they are available, interested, and a good fit for the company," Bill responded.

I told him to vet all the potential applicants and to send in just those he felt were the best candidates. That conversation occurred in the morning.

That afternoon, I received an unexpected call from Ron.

"Jason, hi, it's Ron. The authorities are in the midst of all the interrogations, and I wanted to know if you want to attend one of them. I already asked permission and they told me it would be OK."

"Which one?" I asked.

"George Montry, your CFO. I thought you might want to sit on the other side of the glass and listen in, as well as provide some additional background information as the interrogation progresses. Are you interested?" he asked.

I had to think for a moment about whether I wanted to go through that, but I really wanted to know what had motivated George to turn on me and the company.

"Sure, Ron. And thanks. Just let me know the date, time, and place, and I will be there."

J.T. Palace

A few days later, I was sitting on the other side of one-way glass, along with Ron, an FBI agent, and two police detectives. George was seated in a chair in the interrogation room when a female police detective came in and sat down opposite him. A male detective was standing in a corner, and a man who appeared to be George's attorney was seated next to him.

"Please state your name, home address, and occupation for me," the female interrogator began.

George provided the requested information. He was nervous and sullen, to the point that the interrogator had to repeat some of the questions several times so she could hear and understand his responses.

"When was the first time you had contact with either Herb, Marty, Cal or any of their representatives?" she continued.

"I am not really sure, but I think it was a few months ago," he responded quietly.

"Who was your first contact with?" she asked.

"It was with Cal Donaven, but I only spoke with him once."

"Who were you in contact with later?"

"It was mostly with Marty Gilbert."

"How often were you in contact with him?" she continued.

"At least once a week."

"What did he speak to you about?"

"Initially, he told me why he was calling me, asking me how everything was going, what he wanted, and those kinds of things."

"What was he looking for?"

"Primarily information on how the company was doing, what our plans were, and things like that. Later on, it was more specifically about our steel purchasing, who we bought from, what quantities, what price. Initially, he told me he had some steel vendors that could get us the steel we needed much cheaper than we were paying at the time."

"How did you respond?"

"Wait a minute. You don't have to answer that," George's attorney interceded.

The interrogator got visibly upset. "Counselor, you know that we are trying to ascertain the facts regarding the allegations. Your client has agreed to cooperate with us toward a potential plea bargain. If you want to stop now, your client is most likely looking at about twenty years in prison. Do you want to proceed or not?"

"Go ahead, George," the attorney responded, changing his mind.

"Again, Mr. Montry, what happened in subsequent conversations with Mr. Gilbert?"

"I initially gave him only limited information, but when he told me he could get us less expensive steel, I gave him the information he needed as far as the types of steel, quantities, current prices, the vendors we were using, and that kind of information."

"What did he promise you in return for this information?"

"In the beginning, nothing other than being able to save us money on steel. When I later hesitated to do business with him, he told me he would arrange for any other potential vendor to refuse to sell us the steel. Then he told me that he ultimately planned to take the company back along with Herb, Cal, and some outside partners. He said that the partners would continue to prevent the company from getting any steel until then, and that I was not to even try to buy steel anywhere else. He told me that I would be assured a good place in the company when they took it over, with a ten percent ownership share and substantially higher pay. After he called many times, I finally agreed."

"After you agreed, did anyone else or Marty contact you again?"

"Yes, Marty kept in contact, checking to see if the company had found steel anywhere else, checking on production, those kinds of things."

"How much information did you provide him?"

"I answered his questions, but after a few weeks, I began getting nervous about all this."

"Did you relay that to Marty?"

"Yes, and he told me he would get me some money to relax me, as he called it."

"How much money and in what way?"

"He said he would meet me and give me some cash."

"How much cash?"

"He initially promised me five hundred dollars. When I objected and I told him it was way too low, he kept upping it, finally getting to five thousand dollars."

"When did he give you the money?"

"He never did. I was supposed to meet him a few days ago to get it, but I was arrested."

"Did anyone else contact you besides the initial contact with Cal and all the conversations with Marty?"

"Yes, I got about two, maybe three calls from Herb."

"Herb Henderson?"

"Yes, that is correct."

"What did Herb say?"

"He basically reiterated what Marty had promised me about them taking over the company, my getting a ten percent stake and a very generous salary, those kinds of things."

This continued for two or three hours. The interrogator got into the Russian connection, which George did not know much about. She also tried to pinpoint dates and times of the conversations, and more details about the conversations with Marty, Herb, and the others who had been implicated. George was cooperative, and his attorney only objected a few times. It appeared to me, if I had to guess, that George would receive a minimal sentence under a potential plea bargain, and that Marty and Herb were pretty heavily implicated.

I left the police station with mixed emotions. In one way, I was hurt that George would do this to the company and me. In another way, I was happy it appeared all those involved in trying to destroy and take over the company had been apprehended, accused, and, hopefully, would be tried, convicted, and sentenced to long terms in prison. Finally, I felt that this was my opportunity to move the company forward to where it should be without any outside interference.

I came back to the office just in time to meet Janet Mason, our temporary CFO. I spent about thirty minutes speaking with Jan, bringing her up to date on the company's status, and explaining what her immediate and longer-term duties would be. Jan seemed pleasant enough and had come very highly recommended by Bill. She had bachelor's and master's degrees in business and accounting and finance. She was in her lower forties, about five-foot three-inches tall and slender, with long black hair and a pleasant smile, and she was very serious about her work. She had a good deal of industrial business experience.

"Jan, there are number of things I want you to get to work on right away after you familiarize yourself with our operation. First, we will need you to bring everything up to date, which I believe you have been doing from your office already anyway. Next, I want you to start getting quotes for adding on to our existing building to accommodate the growth we are experiencing currently and that we expect to continue into the foreseeable future," I said.

"No problem. I will get started on these items right away. I am, however, pretty familiar with the company and its operations because I have been working on your account for Bill pretty much since he took it over."

"Great, that will make things much easier. Please keep me abreast of what you are doing. If you have questions, you know where my office is. I will be working on establishing steel suppliers, now that the roadblocks have effectively been removed. Once I have the vendors in place, I will turn them over to you to handle the ordering," I said.

That afternoon and the next day, I spent most of my time on the phone, speaking to old and new potential steel suppliers, starting with Midwest vendors first and then working my way outward to national vendors. In almost every case, once I told them the result of all the company had gone through and provided them the quantities and steel chemistry that we needed, they were eager to give me a quote. After discussing the quotes with Jan, we selected five vendors and gave them sample buys of twenty-five tons each to check on their service and quality. Then we prioritized them based on how they met those criteria. Then we chose the three best. The best one, we gave an order for sixty percent of our requirements. The next, thirty percent. And the last one, ten percent. We also planned to use this latter one to fill in for any sudden increases in requirements that the other two might not be able to meet.

With that completed, I told Jan to begin placing long-term purchase orders, with monthly releases from each. That was our first major hurdle. Next Jan spoke to contractors about a potential building expansion. We estimated we would need to add about 70,000 square feet to our building to cover current needs and projected growth. Jan provided common specifications to each contractor, and each was given thirty days to respond with a quote. In the meantime, we did extensive background checks on the contractors to find out which ones had the best references and experience.

While that was going on, Jan, Katey, and I sat down with Oscar to talk about equipment needs for our current production and products, and what we would need in the near future. He provided us a good deal of input, as always, and then we sat down with our CPAs and attorneys.

Finally, as the quotes came in from the contractors, we again sat down with the accountants and attorneys as well as our bankers to determine the best way to finance this expansion. We had asked five contractors for quotes. It looked like we would need to finance about $10 million for the expansion. The plan was to begin with that amount in the form of a line of credit, with only interest payments. After the construction was complete, we would convert that to a long-term demand note to spread out the payments over about twenty years. At the same time, we could begin ordering equipment for the new addition, and use our machinery and equipment line of credit that would later be converted to a short-term demand note.

It took some heavy discussion to convince our bankers to provide this financing. The biggest problem we ran into was assuring them that the impediments to operating the company properly had finally been removed and that we were in full control. We also spent a lot of time explaining to them the tremendous potential in terms of revenue, cash flow, and profits from our new product line.

We were also in contact with the local planning and building department to make sure the expansion would be approved and that all the paperwork was completed correctly. We all reviewed the five construction quotes. First, we eliminated the lowest one, which was barely half the cost of the middle ones. We knew that any quote so low would be fraught with problems, cost overruns, poor quality, and requests for cost adjustments. Then we looked at the highest quote, compared the details to the others, and realized that the top one was way overpriced. Finally, we looked at the middle three, evaluated how each of the contractors was offering to meet our specifications, and did our own reference checks of projects these three had done in the past three years. We asked customers about quality of work; timeliness of construction deadlines; cost overruns; and how the contractor addressed issues, problems, and corrections. In addition, we checked with our bankers about them.

We finally chose Jason Construction for our project, headed by Albert Jason, the third-generation president of this family-owned business. We were impressed with his knowledge of construction, ease of discussion, willingness to do things the right way, explanation of how the project would progress, and his continuous involvement.

The summer turned to fall and the fall to winter. Although we were in the midst of the expansion, the old adage "stuff happens" proved true time and time again. Late one morning, while finishing some work on the building expansion quotes, my phone rang. It was Pete Lancaster, our shop foreman, who asked me to immediately come out to the production area. Pete was standing in Bay 4 looking up at the ceiling. In reality, he was looking at the sky, and listening to the wind howling outside and inside. We were in the midst of a powerful windstorm that had torn off a portion of our roof. A major snowstorm was forecast for later that evening.

I went to my office and called Tony Badaloucci. Tony was our insurance agent, who specialized in commercial and industrial business insurance coverage and was located in Elizabeth, New Jersey. When I had switched insurance agents a year before, a number of people, including colleagues, friends, and other professionals, had said it was a big mistake because of the lack of proximity to our location. The cost advantages and service recommendations I had received from Tony's office told me otherwise. Now came the real test.

"Hi, Marian. How are you doing today? It's Jason Kirby from Illinois," I began.

"Hi, Mr. Kirby. How are you?"

"I'm fine, thanks. We do, however, have an issue we need addressed immediately. We are in the midst of a major winter windstorm here in Illinois at our facility, and the wind has already torn off part of the roof in the production area of our building. We really need to get someone out here right away to take care of things."

"Tony is out at a client, but I will call the insurance carrier and have them get someone out to your place as soon as possible. We have all your policy and location information here in the office. As soon as I get an estimated time, I will let you know," Marian answered.

"Thanks, but please make this high priority for them."

"I certainly will," she said.

To my amazement, less than three hours later, a repair crew was up on our roof, replacing and securing cross members and metal decking.

When they were done, the crew foreman came in to speak to me. "We have the roof secure and enclosed. You should have no problems with the balance of the windstorm, and no problems with any rain or snow afterward. Our repairs will take care of you for quite a while and will get you through the winter, and as soon the weather clears in the spring, we will return to make final repairs. You should not have any problems until then," he said. "Thank you very much for coming so quickly and completing the repairs. I really appreciate it."

With that, production continued. We never lost a day of work and there was no danger to our employees. My decision to choose Tony's agency proved correct after all. The simple fact is that in business, you never know what is coming next, regardless of extensive planning and analysis. You just have to know how to roll with the punches and deal with matters at hand as best you can, wherever and whenever they occur.

As we were coming to the end of our calendar year, we needed to evaluate our financial situation. Even with all the problems we had experienced launching our new products, struggling to purchase sufficient steel, dealing with the issues with our CFO and outside forces, our volumes and margins had turned out well and we were in a financially secure position.

We knew that although it had involved a great deal of hard work on everyone's part, our plant employees deserved a lot of credit. So Katey, Jan, and I met privately several times to determine exactly how and to what extent we could reward our hard-working employees and not impact the company in a negative manner. We came up with a plan that we implemented on Wednesday, December 23, which would be the last working day for production before the winter holiday shutdown. I arranged for all work to stop at exactly noon, and for all employees to meet in one area of the plant. With microphone in hand, I briefly reviewed the incredible year we were just completing, and some of the trials and tribulations we had gone through, including our proposed building expansion.

"So, in summary, we have all worked very hard to produce quality products, at a fair cost, and in an honest and ethical manner, and to serve our customers quickly and efficiently. The management team and I feel our success is due, to a very great extent, to you, the hard-working employees of our company. I know the past few years have been difficult, and that under the previous management and ownership, you have not had a raise for three years nor have you received a bonus of any sort. Therefore, as your supervisors hand out your regular paychecks today, you will be receiving a second envelope. No, it is not a pink slip. Quite the contrary, the extra envelope is one way that we want to show our appreciation for what you have done, how much we value your work, and how much we want you to remain here as we continue to grow. Everyone who has been working here at least six months will be receiving an additional check in the amount of …" I hesitated for a few seconds to look at the faces in the crowd and see the anticipation, "in the amount of five thousand dollars."

With those last few words came massive applause and shouting amid a sea of smiling faces.

I continued, "Anyone who has been here less than six months will receive a prorated amount of the five thousand dollars based on how long you have been here. Thank you all very much, and I look forward to seeing you all here after January first."

I did not even try to count how many employees came up to give me and the rest of the management team thanks and hugs. Some were simply standing in a state of shock, and others were crying with happiness. Observing all that told me we had done the right thing and were on the right track.

Now it was time to get to work. The next day, I placed a call to Frank at American Steel, to whom I owed a tremendous debt of gratitude and an explanation.

"Frank, how are you doing?" I began.

"I'm fine. How are you?" he responded.

"I'm doing well. I have owed you this phone call for quite some time, but now is the first opportunity I have had to make it. You remember when I asked you to begin shipping us steel, and I told you that as soon as I was able, I would explain exactly why I needed the steel and why my request was under a cloak of secrecy. Well, now I can explain all of it to you."

With that, I explained who had been preventing us from purchasing the steel, and why, and what we had ultimately been able to do about it, and what we were using the steel for. I also explained that we had been able to secure steel on our own from more local sources and in greater quantities than Frank had been able to provide.

"So, Frank, you really came through for us when we needed it, and for that I will be eternally grateful. Whenever you are in town here, I owe you a good dinner."

"Jason," Frank said, "while I will always take a free dinner from you, shipping you this steel does not even repay you one percent for all that you have done for me over the years. I cannot, in fact, ever repay you for all the favors and assistance you have given me in my times of need, but I will still take the free dinner one day. Best of luck, and call me whenever you want, either for some help or just to talk," Frank said.

After we had selected our contractor, we worked with the city council, planning commission, mayor, and other governmental agencies to make sure we had dotted all the i's and crossed all the t's. The planning commission had given us tentative approval to go forward, and the issue was scheduled to come before the city council for approval and public comment. Katey, Mitch, Bill, and I were in attendance, along with Albert and his architect.

When our project came up on the agenda, I walked to the speakers' stand and microphone.

J.T. Palace

"Please state your name, company, and company address for the record." I did and awaited the next question.

"We understand you plan on putting a rather large addition on to your current facility. Can you please explain the nature of this expansion, provide us with some background on the company, what you do, and some details on this expansion?" the council chairman asked.

"Of course," I said. "We are an automotive component manufacturing company. The company has been in business for over fifty years. We have been located in this city for about three years, and we recently have developed and patented some new products and processes that have been accepted very well in the marketplace. As a result, we need to expand our facility to accommodate this increased demand."

The chairman and some of the council members then asked questions, such as the estimated size and cost of the addition, cost of new machinery and equipment that might be needed, new jobs to be created, and so on. I answered each question briefly, with Albert Jason filling in the details.

"We will be adding approximately seventy thousand square feet to our building, at a cost of about ten million dollars. In addition, we expect to purchase and install new machinery and equipment valued in the two to three million dollar range, and create about twenty new jobs initially. If business grows as we anticipate, we would expect the creation of about fifty new jobs in the first two years. Also in response to one of your questions, the operations we will be adding include stamping, welding, metal extrusions, and such. We anticipate the addition to be completed and operational in approximately one year."

Then the chairman called for public comment and questions. There were several questions and comments dealing with minor details, which we quickly answered.

"Can you guarantee me that there will be no impact to the air or water quality in our city as a result of this proposed expansion?" the mayor asked.

"I am sorry. I am not sure what you mean," I said.

The mayor continued. "You know, we have children living in this city, and we need to know that the air and water will not be impacted in any way by your expansion and operations. Can you guarantee me there will be no impact whatsoever?" he asked.

"Sir, we meet or exceed all EPA (Environmental Protection Agency) standards, and any other environmental standards that are part of current law. I cannot guarantee much beyond that," I said.

"But you know, we have our children living here. We cannot risk any impact to them at all," he continued.

"Sir, do you own an automobile?" I asked.

"Yes, of course," he said.

"Do you drive that automobile?" I asked.

"Of course I do."

"Are you concerned about any emissions coming out of the tailpipe of your vehicle, or any of the vehicles of the council members, or of any members of the community?"

"Of course, but I have an electric vehicle. There are zero emissions and zero pollution as a result of my driving my vehicle," he said.

"And do you know where the electricity comes from to charge your vehicle? Do you know what type of power plant is generating the electricity—coal-fired, natural gas, solar, wind, or water? The first two are the predominant power plants the local utilities use in this state currently. Do you think any emissions come out of some of those power plants?"

The mayor went silent at that point. The chairman asked for other questions or comments. There were just a few, and they were quickly answered satisfactorily, and the chairman then asked for a hand and voice vote on our project. Six hands went up, but the mayor kept his hand down. Six sets of eyes stared at the mayor for several seconds, and then he slowly raised his hand slightly. The resolution passed unanimously.

After the meeting, the chairman came up to me along with a few of the council members.

"Sir, I want to apologize for our mayor and his remarks as well as his attitude. He is simply an idiot. This is not the first time he has done something like this." The other council members nodded in concurrence.

"Regardless of what he said, we fully support your project and intend to assist you every step of the way." I thanked them very much and we left the building.

When regular production resumed in January, sales continued to increase, both for the new products we had already introduced and some of the new products we continued to introduce using our proprietary technology. As these sales increases fed into our system, it became more obvious every day that the additional space and equipment were desperately needed, and we continued to move forward with that project. As soon as we had the official city approval, Department of Environmental Quality approval, building permits, and the other requirements that come along with a major project like this, we completed our financing with the bank and began excavation. Footings were poured, water and sewer pipes and gas lines were laid, and the steel people began erecting the steel skeleton, putting the steel cross members and trusses in place. That part of the construction moved quickly, and we were fortunate to have good weather so the construction crews could work consistently. Once the steel was in place, they began the enclosure with additional steel and brick. As that was happening, crews were completing the utility services, including water, natural gas, electrical, and air lines in the ceiling and walls.

The good news about putting an addition on a building that one currently occupies is that you are on-site all the time, observing what the contractors and construction people are doing every day. The downside is that the construction can disrupt day-to-day operations, but we managed. It was exciting to watch the building take shape. We also completed and timed equipment orders for installation.

Of course, while all of this was going on, we had to maintain regular production. That was probably the most difficult part, as resources were stretched thin between supervising the construction project and regular operations.

The months passed quickly as construction moved into the final phases, the concrete floors were poured,

HVAC and lighting was put up, and equipment was installed and tested. We were at production capacity until the addition was completed, which could not come soon enough. Katey was selling our products as fast as they were being introduced, or as the customers required new products using our technology. Oscar was working full tilt making the new products work on a production basis, and we were using Stan and his project management company quite a bit to get us over the hump of introducing the new products and making sure we could produce them quickly and efficiently, at the highest level of quality possible, as well as maintaining our margins. While I was in contact with Albert regularly, he and his crews were doing an excellent job, and I was satisfied we had chosen the right firm.

Chapter 13

Recovery, But at a Cost

Once again, we again began getting strange calls from companies, CPAs, attorneys representing companies, wanting to purchase SMI as it became more apparent that it was expanding and doing well. Many of the callers were just people putting out feelers or representatives looking to make a large commission. When I pressed them for details, they would say they needed to look at our financials, they could not divulge whom they represented, they could not indicate a price range except for such ridiculously high prices they were meaningless. Mitch received similar calls, as did Bill. None of us put much stock in the calls, even though they were getting more frequent, sometimes several in one week.

That is, until one morning I received a very strange call.

"Mr. Kirby?"

"Yes, how can I help you?"

"This is Congressman Balkab from the state of Nebraska. I understand your company is for sale."

"No, that is incorrect; the company is not for sale. Why are you making this call?"

"I am chairman of the United States Congressional Energy and Commerce Committee. We work with a number of companies and foreign governments and have heard that you have received calls from some of the people we work with and have refused to sell your company. Is that correct?"

"Yes, it is. Why? Is that a problem?"

"Well, yes. We certainly don't want to irritate those people in any way, so it might be appropriate if you would reconsider their offers and your position."

"Congressman, with all due respect, I believe this country is still not a dictatorship, and we have the right to accept or refuse offers from any company or country, as we may choose."

"Mr. Kirby, your attitude could have serious repercussions internationally, and I would certainly hope you would reconsider your position. Good day."

With that, he hung up and I was left in shock and disgust.

****

I thought about the conversation and decided to forget it, feeling it may have been from one congressman with some vested interest. I had more important things to worry about, such as completion of construction, installation and startup of the new equipment, building inspection approvals, and so much more.

Then one day, the phone rang, and April told me, "Senator Edwards from Texas is on the phone for you."

"OK, put him through."

"Good morning, Mr. Kirby. This is Senator Mark Edwards, chairman of the United States Senate Foreign Relations Committee. I have been told by Congressman Balkab and others that you have spurned a number of offers from foreign companies and countries to purchase your company. Is that correct?"

"Good morning to you, senator. Before I respond, I would like to know exactly why you are making this call. I didn't know that U.S. senators and congressmen got involved in the business of private companies, particularly when it comes to the operations or purchases and sales of these companies."

"Well, Mr. Kirby, since this involves foreign companies and countries, it comes under the purview of the Senate Foreign Relations Committee."

"Senator, let me stop you right there for a minute." Steam was coming out of my ears, as I was extremely irritated by these U.S. government representatives sticking their noses into our private business, particularly when there were no questions of legality.

"Since we have not discussed nor been involved with any of these foreign companies or countries, nor are we entertaining any offers from these entities, why am I even receiving these calls from U.S. senators and congressmen?"

"Since this can affect our national interest, we make ourselves involved. Now, you say you have not had any offers from these foreign interests. Is that correct?"

"No, I did not say that. I have received numerous phone calls, which I am not the least bit interested in, and U.S. Senate and House members should not be interested in these either, unless any of them have a vested interest in any of these entities."

"Of course we do not, but we are still concerned about the possibilities. I certainly feel you should be entertaining some of these offers."

"Sir, again, with all due respect, this company is not currently for sale, and we do not anticipate it being so for quite some time. So if the United States is still a democracy, and I would appreciate you enlightening me if it is not, we will continue going about our daily business of operating as a business, employing people, and paying taxes, without outside intervention. Would that be OK?"

"We don't want to interfere in your private business, but I am just saying that you should think twice when you receive these phone calls from these foreign entities and maybe entertain some of their offers. It would be in your and the country's best interest. Goodbye." And he hung up.

I could not believe what I had just heard, and I called Bill and Mitch to see if they had received any similar calls. The responses were similar; they had been receiving calls from various company representatives and lower-level congressional representatives regarding a potential purchase, but they were just hypothetical offers with no "real meat" or substance to them. Neither of them had received calls from congressmen or senators to this point, but they agreed that much more was definitely going on than what was on the surface.

I asked each of them to begin checking with any sources they had in the government to see if they could determine who was behind all of this. In the interim, I contacted our Illinois congresswoman, Rep. Dana Sherwood, or attempted to. Her office staff refused to let me speak with her, indicating that I was making something out of nothing and that the senator and congressman who had contacted me were simply doing their jobs. They refused to have Rep. Sherwood call me back.

Next I called one of our senators, Carl Mendoso. After I got through to him, we had a very strange conversation.

"Mr. Kirby, this is Senator Mendoso. How can I help you?" I briefly described what had been going on.

"Can you meet me at the Plaza Garden Park by the water tower in two hours?"

"Of course, I'll be there."

I thought it was a kind of a strange response, but I was determined to meet with him and find out what was going on. Two hours later, I was standing near the water tower waiting for the senator. A few minutes later, he showed up and directed me to sit near a large fountain that was shooting multiple jets of water in predetermined patterns. I thought that was quite odd but walked with him to a spot very close to the fountain. We sat down on a bench next to the fountain, where the water jets were very noisy.

"Mr. Kirby, I chose this location for a reason, but before we have our discussion, please understand that this conversation never happened. I am speaking to you at very high risk, but I believe it is important enough to take this risk. The multitude of noisy water jets in the fountain and the associated colored lights will make it much more difficult for anyone to try to electronically pick up our conversation or read our lips."

His precautions and disclaimers had me concerned for our safety, but I went along because I needed to find out what was going on.

He continued, "I repeat, I want you to understand that this conversation is a great risk to me, but I felt it was important enough to take that risk."

This entire scenario frankly scared me, but I had to continue to find out if my concerns were grounded in fact and how to proceed from here.

Senator Mendoso said, "You are correct. Something is going on, and it reaches to high levels of government and various agencies. The U.S. State Department is and has always been involved in things it should not be. In addition, the Internal Revenue Service is being used as an enforcer in inappropriate and illegal ways. You are getting calls from congressmen and senators because they do, in fact, have vested interests in merger and acquisition activity by foreign individuals, corporations, and countries. As I mentioned, this reaches to high levels of government and has substantially intensified under a recent previous administration that, while it was antibusiness and anti-capitalism, still derives illegal and questionable funding from these same sources and thus worked its way all the way up the line into the White House. What is going on is certainly unethical and, I am firmly convinced, illegal. You should know that you are not alone. There are many people, including myself, at agencies like the IRS, the State Department, in Congress, and even in the White House, who are aware of this activity and are fighting to end it.

"We are going after some of these people one by one, convincing them to stop the activity by, frankly, threatening them with exposure and political destruction with the facts, and in the process, finding out about the next higher level of involvement. It is a slow, risky, dangerous, and tedious process, but it is the only way to finally root out and destroy this disease that is eating up this nation from the inside. In fact, there was a similar situation a number of years ago, when the mayor of a large U.S. city was involved in somewhat similar criminal activity and had his fingers in everything. It took the FBI and many other agencies several years to slowly tighten the rope around his circle of friends, associates and relatives, until they finally had enough hard evidence to bring him to trial, convict him, and incarcerate him for a lengthy period of time. It was a slow, tedious process to close the loop, take out each individual, and slowly close the circle, convicting many along the way. Believe it or not, they are not done with that one, even though it is years later, and are still going after his close relatives and several other associates, but very slowly they are having success. At any rate, this is what we are doing, and I just wanted you to know that you were not alone."

"Senator, I really appreciate your meeting with me and explaining what is going on. I really felt very alone in all of this and was not sure exactly if my assumptions and concerns were correct, let alone what to do about it. This conversation has helped me immensely."

"My pleasure. I really hope it will help you deal with all of this. If you have any other questions or concerns, do not hesitate to contact me. As I mentioned, although we do have people at various agencies and in Congress, one can never be too trusting. In fact, be extremely careful who you do trust."

As I stood up to shake his hand and say goodbye, Senator Mendoso, said, "Wait a minute before you leave. I will leave first. Look carefully at the man in the gray suit over there, that one in the black suit by the light pole, and the one in the dark blue suit over there near the red car. They are all with me and will check the area to make sure you are not being followed. When they give you a nod, you can safely leave as well. Goodbye for now." He left and joined the three men, who then each nodded to me to indicate it was all right for me to leave as well.

As I drove back to the office, my head was spinning. In my mind, I was replaying all that the senator had told me, while at the same time wondering who was involved in this giant criminal conspiracy, and exactly what to do about it from the company's perspective. I knew the calls would continue, and I had to have a reasonable response each time to fend them off, hopefully permanently. The calls did continue, as did my calls to senators, congress people, and anyone else I could find to shed some light on all of this. Some of my inquiries provided positive responses, some were very negative, and some were simply a waste of time.

I became more irritated and concerned as the days went by. One day, April brought my mail in as usual, and as I scanned through the envelopes, one caught my eye. It was a small, plain, white envelope marked "Personal and Confidential." There was no return address, and as I was about to put it in the junk/shredding pile, I changed my mind and opened it.

The short, hand-printed message simply said, "Meet me at the church in town on Eighth Street and Palton at 8:00 p.m. on Thursday for answers to your questions."

Given that it was only Tuesday, I folded the letter back up and set it aside, uncertain as to what to do. Who was this from? What did he or she want? Was this legitimate? Was this dangerous? Was my life at risk? Question after question flew through my mind, so I decided to forget about it for a day or two, hoping clarity or answers would come to me.

The time passed quickly, and suddenly it was Thursday afternoon. I took the letter out of my drawer and reread it several times, still not knowing what to do. Showing up at the church could put me in a risky situation or maybe no one would be there. Against my better judgment, I decided to head over to the church that evening.

It was already dark when I drove up to the church on Eighth Street. I was about ten minutes early, so I decided to wait in my car and get the lay of the land. The area appeared deserted at first, but then a few pedestrians went in and out of the nearby restaurants and bars, and a few cars passed.

I mustered up my courage and stepped out of the car, heading directly to the front door of the old church. I opened the massive wooden door, entered the church, walked down the aisle, and sat down in one of the pews, about in the middle of the church.

After just a few minutes, a skinny man wearing a dark brown hooded jacket sat down next to me and handed me a folded piece of paper. I looked down at it and tried to read it, but it was quite dark and I could barely make out the words. All I could see were a few numbers and letters, as well as the words "Twenty Fourth Avenue main."

"This is all you will need," he said as I looked at the paper again.

I turned toward him and asked, "What does this mean?"

But he had disappeared.

The church was as silent and empty as it had been when I entered. I cautiously walked out, looking all around and behind me, and got in my car. I opened the small folded piece of paper again trying to figure out what it meant, and then I slowly drove home, not understanding what had just happened, let alone what was written on the paper.

By the time I got home and had dinner, the local evening news had come on the television, and as I half-listened, still pondering the note, I caught the newscaster mentioning that a man in a dark hooded jacket had apparently jumped from the Market Street Bridge downtown. Police divers were searching the river below but had not found the man. Could this be the man I had met in the church this evening?

It seemed like just a coincidence until the next morning's news. The announcer said police had found a dark brown hooded jacket floating downriver from the bridge but still had seen no sign of the man eyewitnesses said had jumped or fallen from the bridge the night before. The announcer also said police divers were back in the water this morning, but so far no body had been found. To me, this all seemed to fit together, and I assumed the man who I had met had to be the same as the one that had jumped off the bridge.

But why? Was he being chased? Was this a suicide? Was he pushed? Was this planned or was someone trying to kill him because of the information he possessed? Was his death related to the note he had given me? Or was I just jumping to conclusions? I had so many unanswered questions. And there was still the note. What did it mean? I read it yet one more time. All that was written was "921 Bur," and "Twenty Fourth Avenue main." What could that mean, and why had he said that it was all I needed? Why did he even give this note to me? I put the note in my pocket and drove to the office to deal with the issues of the day.

On my drive in, I listened to the car radio to catch various news broadcasts. I picked up a few more details but none that answered my questions:

"This morning, police divers located a dark brown hooded jacket, believed to have been worn by the man who is believed to have jumped off the bridge last night. Thus far, no body has been recovered. Police think that currents may have pulled him down to the bottom or carried him farther down the river. The search will continue, at least for the next day or two." All day, amidst the phone calls, emails, meetings, and regular day-to-day problems, the letter and the hooded man were on my mind.

What could the words on the note mean? Why had he disappeared so quickly from the church? Why did he choose me to give the note to? Exactly what did the words in the note mean, and why did he say that it was all I needed to know? I was in a meeting with Katey when suddenly it dawned on me.

"Katey, I know what the note means. I have to go. I will see you later," I said, and I shot out of the office and headed to the city's main library. Katey had no clue what I was talking about and did not say a word as I flew past her. I got to the library within thirty minutes and went directly to the adult reading section and looked in the nonfiction area of biographies.

"Seven hundred to nine hundred, nine hundred to eleven hundred." I turned down that row. "Nine hundred, nine hundred ten, nine hundred twenty, nine hundred twenty one. Nine hundred twenty one A... B... BA... BE... BI... Bur. Nine hundred twenty one Bur."

I had realized the hooded man's note was a reference to the Dewey Decimal System used to file books in most libraries. Based on the number and letters, it referred to a biography of someone whose name began with "Bur." I quickly went up and down the rows, finally finding what I was looking for. A biography number 921, Bur was for Thomas Burkhart. I took it off the shelf and read the back cover.

"The story of a titan of the twentieth century, beginning with a small scrap metal yard where he worked as a young man and working his way up to general manager, young Thomas Burkhart eventually purchased the company from the owner. Then it was more local scrapyards, which quickly became scrapyards across the country, then smelting furnaces, and finally metals commodities. Thomas Burkhart Sr. died in 1948, shortly after World War Two, during which he had made millions of dollars selling to the United States military."

"Wait, that can't be right," I thought. That was so many years ago…

Then I read on. "Young Thomas Burkhart Jr. took over the reins of the company from his father and rapidly expanded his empire into aluminum, uranium, and lithium mines all over the world. As tough as Thomas Burkhart Sr. was, young Thomas Jr. was much more successful and much more ruthless, eventually creating and growing this empire into International Resources, a global commodities powerhouse."

I flipped through the book. Inside were several pages of notes, handwritten on notebook paper. I took them out and put them in my pocket and took the book to the checkout, scanned the bar code, and took it home to read. I had a quick dinner with my wife and explained that I had to go into my home office to read a book. As daylight began to appear, I completed the book, fascinated by what I had read and intrigued by how it related to the notes I had found inside. The notes consisted of dates, times, names, locations, conversations and events revolving around John Burkhart Sr. and Jr., congressmen, senators, the attorney general's office, the State

Department, FBI, CIA, global leaders, all the way up to and throughout the White House.

While I had half-expected something like this, I was stunned at the magnitude and depth of participation of those involved. I waited a short time to absorb all that I had read. I realized that I knew exactly what I had to do, and decided to begin the next day after I got some rest. I called the office and left a message for Amy that I would be coming in late that morning.

I got a few hours of sleep and went to the office to carry on my normal duties without sharing any of what I had read or the events of the prior evening. I knew it was best not to even hint at what I knew. Later that evening, I made some copies of the notes on my home printer and some phone calls. For the next few days I met, either in person or by phone, with the editors of several local and national newspapers, recording the conversations and letting the editors know of the recordings. I made sure that associate or assistant editors were also present during these conversations.

Then I made one additional call. "Can I speak to Senator Mendoso, please?"

"May I ask who is calling?"

"Yes, it is Jason Kirby."

"One moment, please."

"Jason, how are you?" the senator asked when he came on the line.

"Senator, I need to see you right away. Where and when can we meet?" I asked.

"Ah, meet me at the entrance to Jasper Square in Allison, Illinois, at two p.m. today," he offered. "Will that be OK?"

"I'll be there, thank you." And I hung up. This had to be done immediately.

At one fifty that afternoon, I parked at the entrance to the park and got out. I walked over to the gate, went inside, and waited. A few minutes later, the senator walked in, along with some of his security team, who stayed within about a fifty-foot perimeter.

"Jason, I know you would not have asked me to come so quickly if it wasn't important. What have you got?"

"I have some copies for you to look over, but I want to explain a few things first. I received this from a young man who was privy to a great deal of information and who arranged for me to have these notes, although I don't know why. They name names, places, events, and everything else regarding what we have been discussing recently and what you have been working on. I just want you to know that I cannot continue dealing with all the senators and congressmen pressuring me to sell my company to foreign entities; the constant flow of people calling me, my attorneys, and CPAs, trying to purchase the company; and the veiled threats. I know there needs to be an end to all of this, and that time is now."

"As I said, I am giving you a copy of these notes for you to do what you need to do. I want you to know that I have provided these notes to the editors of several local and national newspapers with the following instructions: They are to publish this information in thirty days unless any of the following things happen: First, if I call them before that time indicating they should not publish the information or, second, if I call them to let them know to release the information earlier, or third, if anything happens to me, they are instructed to publish this information immediately. Now I want you to look over all of this very quickly while I am here with you. This will give you thirty days to present this information to the appropriate parties and let them know that newspapers will be publishing it in the time frame I indicated. You can make it clear to the people involved that they can go public in advance, resign, turn themselves in, or work out plea deals, whatever you want, but they and their associates and accomplices will be implicated and prosecuted to the full extent of the law for what they have done."

The senator took the copies I handed him, reviewed them quickly, and stood silently, shocked at the revelations they contained.

"Thank you. This is incredible and exactly the kind of information we have been looking for and trying to assemble for a long time. It will make our job much easier to accomplish. I will definitely get back to you prior to the thirty days endpoint. Goodbye and good luck. You have performed a tremendous service to your country and to me."

With that, the senator turned and left, along with his security team, although they indicated again they would watch me until I left, for my own safety.

The days passed quickly as I was heavily involved in day-to-day operations, completion of our expansion, and getting new products into production. Always in the back of my mind, though, was the ticking clock, waiting for the thirty days to elapse, waiting to see articles in the paper related to those who were implicated in this giant conspiracy and, in addition, waiting to hear anything about the young man in the hooded jacket. I wanted to know if he had been found or not, if he was safe or not.

Periodically, I noticed little articles in the newspaper in places that most people would not look. Things like, "Congressman Matthews from Missouri suddenly resigned with no explanation other than to say he needed to take care of personal matters." And another saying, "Senator Kranoff from Vermont resigned effective in two weeks to pursue other opportunities." Interestingly, most of these were small articles relegated to page 12 in section B in some newspaper, with barely a mention on radio or television. Senator Mendoso also called occasionally to keep me up to date on his actions and pending announcements that I would hear about in a day or two.

Then a stunning story hit the front pages as well as broadcast media: indicated that "After a federal grand jury in Washington DC had been empowered recently by a local prosecutor in a federal district court, indictments had been handed down by that same grand jury."

"United States Attorney General Hal Erickson has resigned after being indicted on charges of gun running, money laundering, fraud, conspiracy, misfeasance and malfeasance, perjury, and other crimes."

Another article said, "Treasury Secretary Gene Thomas has been indicted for failure to pay income tax, tax fraud, failure to report income, and tax evasion."

Then came an article about the secretary of defense, Herbert Charles, being indicted "for perjury in front of the United States Senate Armed Forces Committee, for passing defense secrets to foreign governments, and other more detailed charges."

Then the biggest story of all: The grand jury had "brought down indictments against the vice president and president of the United States for perjury in front of a Senate committee, money laundering, misfeasance and malfeasance, and accepting bribes and payoffs." The list went on and on. The story continued to unfold. A few days later the president of the United States accepted the resignation of his vice president, pending anticipated charges of fraud, conspiracy, and blackmail involving several congressmen, senators, and some foreign leaders.

Not only did that send Washington abuzz; it also prompted a call from Senator Mendoso to me late one evening.

"Jason, a group of senators and congressmen from both parties were called into the Oval Office today by the president. He was very concerned about what was going on around him, and wanted to know how to avoid additional public announcements of the scandal that is being uncovered and may have involved him. He was very concerned that items would leak out, such as his approval of over a billion dollars of taxpayer money given to a company for a supposed environmentally sound technology, when it was really a payoff to friends and party supporters. He was also concerned that the public would find out he had lied and falsified documents showing that he was qualified to be the president of the United States when, in fact, he was not. In addition, he suggested he had not been entirely truthful and forthcoming, particularly with the public and the media about legislation and agreements with foreign countries that he had supported. He hinted he might have had some association with all of this and was looking for a face-saving way out. Fortunately, as you are now aware, a few months ago we found a judge and subsequently a federal prosecuting attorney in the Washington area to pursue individuals who were involved in all of this, but that may take some additional time. We have now created a federal grand jury to investigate all of this and ultimately to bring down indictments. I will keep you up to date, but this is the beginning of the end of the current administration and all the dirty things they have done. We are still waiting to hear about the foreign companies, and we have to work out the cleanup and replacements for all of these individuals, carry out prosecution, and all of the other details. This is all thanks to you. I and this country are indebted to you."

I said, "I am just glad you have been successful and this is ultimately coming to a positive conclusion, so we can get on with our lives and get this country back on track."

I followed the events in the newspapers and watched with a chuckle as the stories dominated the front page day after day. Some congressional representatives who had been implicated in the affair committed suicide, but most resigned. Even more interesting were the announcements from the foreign press involving prime ministers, foreign ministers, corporate CEOs and presidents of large companies in Europe, Africa, and the Far East.

As my thirty-day deadline approached, the biggest announcement of all came suddenly in a news bulletin one evening. "White House Press Secretary Albert Whitehall has just announced that the president of the United States has resigned his office effective immediately for personal reasons. Due to other resignations and indictments, Speaker of the House Margaret Simonson will be acting president until the next election."

The saga was nearing its conclusion. The next day, I received a call from Senator Mendoso. "Jason, can you meet me next Monday at my office in Washington? I need to speak to you about a few things."

"Sure, what time do you want me there?"

"How about eleven in the morning?"

"Fine, I will arrange for a flight down and I'll be there." I did not know why he wanted me to meet with him, but I felt after all he had done for me, it was appropriate for me to go.

That call came on Tuesday afternoon, barely a week after the last announced resignation. That afternoon, April brought my mail in to me. In the pile was a small envelope, with no return address and no discernible postmark. I opened it and found one piece of lined paper with a brief hand-printed message: "Thanks. You handled the information perfectly. All is taken care of. I am doing fine. Hope to see you one day again. Thanks again."

I smiled and felt good. The letter had no signature and no other identifying marks, but I was absolutely sure I knew who it was from. I was happy to know he was safe and well.

The following Monday came very quickly. I flew down to D.C. to meet with Senator Mendoso, and a taxi took me to the entrance of his building. I paid the driver, stepped out of the taxi, and headed toward the front entrance.

I announced myself to the receptionist and was immediately escorted into the senator's office.

"Hi, I am here to see Senator Mendoso."

"Please come right in." I was escorted to the senator's inner office.

"Would you like something to drink—bottled water, coffee, tea, juice?"

"Just some cold water will be fine, thanks," I responded. In just a minute, Senator Mendoso came in and sat down next to me.

"Jason, it is so good to see you. I don't even know where to begin, but let me start by telling you thank you very much for all you have done, for me, for the nation, and for the United States government. I also want you to know that because of your actions, many people will be made to account for their transgressions and violations of the law, the public trust and, where appropriate, they will be made to pay for those actions both monetarily and with incarceration. We are all indebted to you."

I said, "Thanks, but what I did was only part of the entire episode. I am very glad this issue is being resolved properly and certainly hope that the new people coming into office will make sure it does not happen again and will begin to steer the nation on the right path."

Then the senator got down to the nitty-gritty of things. "Now, I didn't ask you to fly down just to thank you. Frankly, I could have done that on the phone. The truth is, we could really use you in the government to help with this transformation."

"I am not sure I understand what you are saying, Senator. You and your colleagues who were elected to office are here to make sure we are on the right course. Why would you need me?" I asked, a little puzzled.

Then I learned the true nature of my visit. "As you know, there are many areas of government where there is a considerable amount of graft, corruption, and bribery, not to mention the lack of efficiency and tremendous waste. Programs like Medicare, military procurement, the IRS, the State Department, just to name a few, have been rife with corruption, lack of efficiency and, I am sorry to say, lack of competence. We could certainly use someone with your talents and capabilities to clean this up and steer the ship straight, onto a new course. We—*I* would like you to join this effort and head some of these agencies to correct some of these weaknesses. Will you join us?"

I was stunned. I had not anticipated his request in any way and had no idea how to answer. I sat for a moment or two, and then began my response. "Senator, I am certainly flattered that you regard me as so capable, but I just run a small manufacturing company. I have no political expertise or experience. Besides that, our company is growing, and now that some of these diversions are not present anymore, we have much to do to continue to grow the company and prepare for the future. I really could not take on something like this."

"Jason, I fully understand, but you are more than capable, and you are exactly the kind of person we have been looking for to help us with these issues. We really need you."

"Well, how about if I answer you in a kind of different way? I am not saying no, just saying not now."

"I will take that for now, but you are not off the hook. I will be contacting you on a regular basis in the future, asking the same question, and will not take no for an answer indefinitely, and will not even take 'not now' for an answer for very long."

We exchanged some pleasantries, spoke about the economy and some of the issues at the various agencies he had mentioned, and agreed to talk on a regular basis. He also updated me on the investigation and all the people who were involved in the corruption we had just finished eliminating. I said goodbye, was escorted back to the entrance of the building, and provided a car and driver to take me back to the airport.

On the flight, I thought about my conversation with the senator, the progress the company was making, and a million other things. All of a sudden, I heard a voice, "Please fasten your seat belts and place your seats in an upright position. We will be landing at Springdale International Airport in a just a few minutes …" I had drifted off and now was about to return to reality.

After landing, I drove directly to the office. I had much to do and precious little time to do it. After arriving, I was briefed by my executive team on a number of issues and questions I had. Soon I would have to make some major decisions about the company and my life, and I needed as much information as possible. The balance of the day went by quickly, as did the succeeding ones.

The calls about selling the company had essentially ended, except for the "normal" ones that any growing company experiences. As business continued to grow and we occupied and used more of our building addition and new equipment, we also hired more production employees and evaluated whether we needed additional midlevel management to deal with this growth. We did continue to use some consulting assistance in the interim to get us over this hump.

One day, April brought in the mail as usual. I was on the phone and flipped through the pile quickly as always. One letter caught my attention, but I did not have time to look at it until later in the day. Around three in the afternoon, I came back to my office and sat down at my desk. I had a few minutes to look through the mail again, and I saw the envelope I had noticed earlier in the day. It was a plain white envelope with no return address. Inside was a white piece of paper with a brief message apparently printed on a computer printer.

It simply said,

"WE ARE DOWN BUT NOT OUT. WE WILL BE BACK"

About the Author

J.T. Palace worked in education, manufacturing, and government in the Midwest before retiring and starting the writing career that had been a lifelong dream. The impetus for this story is to show what really happens in the business world, but in a more dramatic, fictional way. Palace also enjoys travel, photography, and home maintenance.

Made in the USA
Middletown, DE
22 November 2021